LEGEND OF NOW

Copyright © 2024 E. Merwin
& Julie Carter Merwin

Artwork by J. Carter Merwin
ISBN: 9780578444062

 Braiswick

First published by Braiswick
Felixstowe, England, 2015.

Editor: Trevor Lockwood

www.emerwin.com

LEGEND OF NOW

BY

E. MERWIN

ARTWORK BY

F. CARTER MERWIN

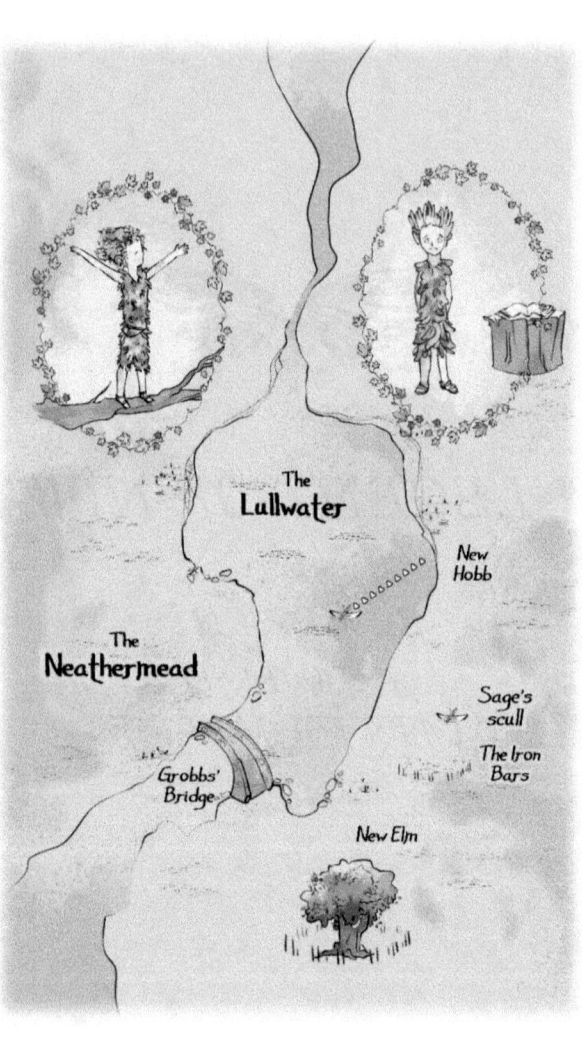

The
Lullwater

New
Hobb

The
Neathermead

Sage's
scull

The Iron
Bars

Grobbs'
Bridge

New Elm

CONTENTS

ACKNOWLEDGMENTS

With endless thanks to Trevor Lockwood of Felixstowe England—writer, publisher & literary friend—for his bright mind, good works, and generous encouragement.

CHAPTER ONE

To begin, Indigo is much like you—highly curious, fiercely independent and if treated unfairly, she does get angry. One difference? Height. The smallest leaf on the elm above would be to her as wide as an umbrella. Right now Indigo is locked inside the tree and forbidden to leave the courtroom until dismissed by Chief Justice Bitterroot. Rising from the acorn-carved chair, she wipes the beads of bluish perspiration from her brow. Then loudly enough to vent her anger, lowly enough not to wake the cold-blooded chief justice who is dozing at his desk, she grumbles.

"No way. No how. Not now. Not ever!"

Indigo creeps past him toward the ivy curtained knothole. When she pulls aside the leaves in streams a lemony light flecked with pollen grains and spores. Indigo glances back to check that the lizard is not spying on her through his dark, orange-rimmed eyes.

Stretching upward, she grabs hold of the bark sill and flails from side to side to gain momentum until throwing a leg outside the tree, Indigo faces the sky. With her hair a mass of twisting blue tendrils, she gazes over the Nethermead where They lounge on blankets like lizards on stones. One of Them flicks a red saucer across the field which glides into the jaws of its Beast that leaps to catch it between its teeth. When it runs to drop the disk at its master's feet and barks, the other says, "Good job."

"Good job!" echoes Indigo who barks into the canopy of an elm tree in Prospect Park so historic that it has been surrounded by an iron fence. Built to stop any human eager to carve their initials into its sapwood or hang from its branches, it is no barrier to the beetles, bats, rats, ants, birds and other creatures that Indigo has befriended.

Taking hold of a stem of ivy, she prepares to climb. With her robe of fallen leaves, sewn with the shimmering threads of a spiderweb, flapping in the breeze, she struggles to rise onto a narrow branch where she stands beside a sparrow and stares up into its dark eye.

"Really, like what's the point?"

The head of the bird turns to follow the flight of a passing dragonfly.

"We can't enchant humans anymore, we can't even mess up their day. And don't even think about life in the Old Order. Oh no, that would be breaking Law 672: think no thought of the ancestors without prior permission." Leaning closer, she adds with a wink. "But I do."

From the bird's throat rise three bright notes.

"You really want to know? Simple. I shift. If the law says: no dipping, no diving, no flitting, no flying, back then we probably did. Or else why would they have passed a law against it?"

The bird studies the chittering creature—too big to be eaten, too small to be a threat. "Back in the day, we must have flit, flown, dipped and dived as much as we wanted. But no, not now. Why?" With a shrug she mutters in disgust. "We're Priggs. I'm Priggish."

An angry face of shifting shades of peach and honey, topped with a shock of equally bright bristles, pops out of the hollow and searches the branches. The creature hisses just loudly enough to be heard above the snores that echo inside the trunk. "Indigo. What are you doing

3

up there?"

"Just chilling."

"Chilling?"

"You know, hanging out with my new friend." Indigo reaches up to pat the tip of the brown and red wing of the bird that warbles into the treetops.

"No, I don't know. Besides, that bird doesn't understand a word you're saying."

"Like any of you do?"

"Well, at least I understand we're on Alert Level 3. Nobody, not even the servants are allowed outside."

"So?"

"So?" replies Thistle, deeply disturbed by Indigo's blatant disregard of the clear and present danger facing the New Order of the World. "Two of their drooling Beasts were spotted last night sniffing around the Iron Bars, right below where you happen to be sitting— illegally!"

"Technically, I'm still on the tree."

"Yes, but you're not in it, and if Bitterroot wakes up, you'll get us both grounded!"

"Grounded? Our whole life in this crooked old tree is grounded!" Indigo arches her back and tips her face toward the sun. "Out here I feel free!"

"Free to be what? Blown away forever?"

"Maybe I'd like that. When I stand here like this, I feel kind of, well, possible."

"Possible?"

"Yes, possible. Like I can be or do anything. Like I have two huge wings, and I can fly anywhere I want. Like our ancestors used to."

"They were Sprites, Indigo, and you're not!"

Taking a deep breath, she inhales the moist air and smells the zing of an oncoming rain.

"Thistle, don't you ever wish?"

"I never wish, and neither should you!"

"Then how can you ever understand who I am on the inside?"

With a bounce the bird flies off, catapulting the twig-like Prigg into the air. "Look, Thistle, I'm..." Gravity snatches a word midair as Indigo falls and her sandals fly upward.

Thistle gasps to see two bits of bark tossed about by the breeze while barefoot Indigo clings to a stem directly above the spikes of the Iron Bars. Just beyond the knothole, a bee holds its position to observe this scene while its buzzing wings distort Thistle's cry. "Hold on. I'll get Martine!"

High above the courtroom on the judge's bench, Bitterroot still slumbers. The sound of his snoring diminishes as Thistle glides past him and down the polished hardwood floors. Zigzagging through the maze of corridors, he scans the walls. From the shadowy ceiling, a pair of green bulging eyes follow the frantic Prigg who catches sight of the mantis.

"Quick, Martine, it's Indigo. She's in danger."

The insect flies to the ground in a spiraling pattern. It lands beside Thistle and tilts its heart-shaped head to ask, where?

"Outside and do hurry, we're on Alert Level 3!"

The mantis lowers its leaf-like body for Thistle to climb on its back then gallops down the halls and into the law chamber. As Thistle slides to the ground, he presses his hands together, interlocking his long fingers and squeezing them until they turn a bright orange. When Martine steps outside, he rotates his head 180 degrees to scan the air, alive with buzzing insects and distant voices. A gray squirrel, its cheek bulging with an acorn, scrambles up the trunk and locks its eyes on Indigo.

When Martine leaps onto a limb far below where Indigo dangles, Thistle squeals a high-pitched note, a long barely audible *eee*. "No, Martine, higher, higher!"

The squirrel spits out the nut and moves closer to the dangling Prigg. When its whiskers brush against Indigo's squirming toes, her grip on the stem weakens.

"Uh, help?" she murmurs while directly below them the mantis hisses with fury and fans out its wings. The startled rodent jumps from the branch, launching its prey into Martine's raised raptorial forelegs.

Indigo plants a kiss beneath the insect's mandibles then straddles its back to ride up the bark, through the knothole and onto a patch of moss where Thistle stands fuming. His pale skin reddens which gives him the fiery glow of a struck match as he scolds. "Are you crazy? What if you fell, what if a Beast came along?"

"What if—you're always worrying about what if. Thistle, think about it. What if something wonderful happens?"

"Wonderful is against Law 947 And so is thinking!"

Thistle's agitated voice startles the chief justice who wakes and mutters, "Uh yes, quite correct. Strictly illegal."

The lizard squints into the stream of light that pours through the knothole, uncertain of the identity of the radiant silhouettes until Indigo steps into view and addresses him with a smirk. "Asleep at the switch again, eh, Bitterroot?"

"What Indigo means, Chief Justice," stammers Thistle, approaching the desk.

"I am accustomed to Indigo's disrespect as well as her utter disregard for education."

"Well maybe, Bitterroot, I just have some different ideas."

"There will be no different ideas in the New Order of the World. And no discussion." With the sharpened tip of a quill, he scratches the scaly bump above his reptilian eyes and leers at the yawning young Prigg. "Now to conclude. Indigo, what is the next to last law of the New Order?"

"Next to last, first, they're all the same. We can't do or be anything!"

"Enough!" shouts the chief justice. "Those are forbidden words for any Priggish citizen, especially a member of the first family whose only concern should be the N.O.W. exam."

"I'm sick of hearing about that stupid exam. What if I don't want to take it?"

"But you have to pass it to get into Dale," pleads Thistle, who having been appointed as Indigo's tutor is responsible for her score. "Not take the New Order of the World Exam? For you, that's not possible."

"Possibly, I'll not show up. Trust me, I can find something better to do with my time."

Bitterroot rises and slashes the air with a long, curved claw. "There is nothing better, nothing more important than the study of law. It is the cornerstone of our society. The way we conduct Priggish business, protect our citizens, and control all the other creatures whose work is essential to our wellbeing."

"Our wellbeing? What about theirs? And protect us from what? And maybe nobody in the New Order needs to be controlled."

"Oh but, Indigo, we all must be controlled." Nervously Thistle clenches the brightening fingers of his left hand with the right. "For our own safety."

"You see, even Thistle understands our Priggish principles." With a fake smile Bitterroot pokes his fingers into Thistle's tall bristles and gives a shake, making the sound of wind rattling tall, dry grasses. "Not a drop of blue blood flowing in his veins, and yet he obeys."

Thistle bows his head in shame toward the mossy floor as Indigo climbs onto the judge's bench and admires her lavender toes.

"Yo, Bitterroot, word on the street? Orange? It's the new blue." Indigo winks at Thistle who hides a shy smile behind his tangerine fingertips while Bitterroot scowls, his brow resembling a dried-out riverbed with his wart, a barren island at its center.

"Get down from there instantly! And cease in the usage of those hideous phrases you pick up eavesdropping on Them in the park."

"I can't help it if people are loud. Anyway, why can't I express myself around here?"

"Oh, Indigo, you know that's against the law."

"Oh, Thistle, but why?"

A buzzing reverberates off the curved wall. The governor's bee flits in and waggles a dance-like pattern. On the Nethermead waggling is its way to inform other bees of a good source of nectar, but here in the elm of the New Order, its messages inform on the whereabouts of all Priggs.

"Uh-oh, here comes the snitch."

Bitterroot glares at Indigo. "Bizby reports that you were recently sighted on the uppermost branch."

"Tell Bizby to read my lips." Indigo mouths three syllables: I don't care.

"As your mother, the governor, is awaiting our arrival in her chamber, perhaps you can tell her that yourself."

"Don't worry, I will."

When Bitterroot snaps his fingers and points to the ground, the mantis obeys. "I will ride while you, Indigo, follow." The lizard mounts and digs a toe into Martine's abdomen.

Thistle leans toward his student and whispers. "But, Indigo, what about the four?"

"Don't worry, four or no four, I can handle the governor."

"Silence. Thistle, your tutorial services are hereby terminated. I am demoting you to the compost heap. Report to the root cellar." With a flick of his long sticky tongue, the chief justice snatches a gnat from the air which he munches loudly while Thistle gathers up his books with trembling hands.

Meanwhile Indigo stands in the doorway, whistling and waiting until the chief justice has ridden down the long passageway. After his image has merged with the shadows, she gives Thistle an illegal hug. "Remember what tomorrow is?"

Thistle pushes her away. "No!"

"Come on, it's my birthday. And yours."

"And remembering them is strictly prohibited."

"Well, I do."

"Just because we happen to be born on the same day, don't go dragging me into your unlawful enthusiasm.

You're a somebody, I'm a nobody. But once your mother finds out about the four, we're probably both doomed."

"Don't sweat it, Thiz. You know what they used to say in Old Elm. All's well that ends well." Thistle plugs up his ears and scowls. "At least that's what Pop says they used to say." Indigo steps into the corridor and rises on tiptoe.

With her slender arms shooting upward like stems toward the sun, she faces its imaginary light and leaps headlong into the darkness.

CHAPTER TWO

The whir of wings fills the Upper Office and flutters the documents on the desk where the governor sets down her quill, rises and smooths the folds of her feather and fern robe. "Show them in when they arrive. And next time, Bizby, clean yourself off before entering my chamber."

Sticking out its tongue, the bee moistens its foreleg

and brushes the bright powder from its head into the pollen basket on its hind legs.

"That's more like it. And remember, your duties are here in my chamber, not lollygagging outside in some clump of wildflowers."

The bee wipes off a few more grains from its thorax as the governor's husband grips the long, tapered end of a twig, flexing his knees before tapping a polished white pebble into a hollow kernel of corn under the desk.

"Winston, put away those clubs before Indigo arrives." The governor crosses to a knothole where a spike of lavender dries out in the sun. She plucks a flower which she crushes between her palms, then with a fingertip rubs its oil into her temples to calm her agitated nerves.

"Now, dear, you know how emotional you get, so please go easy on her."

"Easy? Go easy? Sometimes you sound more like a Sprite than a Prigg! Just look at the way you play that silly game day in and day out."

"Winnie, you know perfectly well that golf is not a game. It is a method of diplomacy between colonies. And I am practicing my diplomatic skills to help us negotiate with the duke for better terms in hiring his daughter."

"Well, New Hobb is up to its ears in debt. On top of his own years of extravagance, her tuition at Dale has left him with an astounding debt. I have no doubt we can get her for a song."

"A song, my dear? Isn't that word a bit, shall we say, Old Elmish."

"Quite right, Winston, and as such prohibited. I meant to say cheap price."

Bizby waggles in the doorway to indicate the direction from which the chief justice is approaching before flying through a knothole for some more lollygagging on the Nethermead.

While Bitterroot bows and stumbles, Martine scales the wall to cling to the ceiling. "Good evening, Governor."

"That all depends on your report, Chief Justice. What is Indigo's score?"

Bitterroot scratches his wart nervously. "Her score, Madam Governor?"

"Yes, out with it."

"In the range, Madam Governor, of a four."

The governor's face shifts to a livid shade of sky blue, and her voice becomes slow and dangerous. "Four hundred out of 1,999 laws? Do you mean to stand here and tell me that a child of the first family barely scored 20%?"

"No, Governor, not 20%."

"Are you suggesting that I am incapable of basic mathematical estimation?"

Indigo saunters in. "What Bitterroot is trying to tell you, Mother, is that I didn't score four hundred. I scored four."

"You scored what?"

"Four, Mother. Yes, a four."

"If I may say so, Governor," interrupts the chief justice.

"No, you may not! Now out of my sight. Go to your chamber until you are summoned."

The chief justice scutters into the corridor where he remains in the shadows to lurk and listen as the governor falls heavily into the chair at her desk and groans. "A four? Indigo, you know that to be even considered for Dale you need a 1600 minimum!"

"Whatever." Indigo reaches for one of her father's golf clubs and examines the ring of blue crystals that encircle the tip of its grip. "Did your clubs really come from Old Elm, Pop?"

"Actually, Indigo, these were passed down to your great-great-grandmother Zinnia. She, that is to say my line of the family, had migrated from Scotland to England back in the 1500s and when they did, they brought with them this beautiful game."

"What's so beautiful about knocking a pebble around with a twig?"

"Ah, back in the day we, I mean they," he corrects himself under the stern gaze of his wife. "They played in the open air—along rabbit runs, across sand dunes, braced by a brisk Scottish breeze. And so, it caught on in jolly Old Elm—that is until she and the King set sail."

"But if it was so jolly, why did she leave?"

Winston does not answer. Instead, he takes hold of the antique club by its shaft and raises it toward the late afternoon light that slants through the knothole. He sighs as he admires the dull glow of its blue Derbyshire crystals. "Now that, my dear, is a bit of a mystery."

Indigo widens her eyes and puffs up her cheeks as she exhales heavily. "Everything about Old Elm is a mystery."

"Well, some mysteries are just secrets, but in this case, we really can't be sure why she chose to leave. You see, Zinnia had been quite the athlete and something of a poet as well. But then somehow her point of view shifted. She set to work writing restrictive laws, 2,000—well, to be exact 1,999 as the last was somehow lost—and then set off in the hold of a ship with her husband the King to create a New Order of the World."

"A boring order."

"A better order" snaps the governor. "A more efficient order, an order without all the nonsense of magic, pranks and all that time wasted on fiddling about. A new order founded on neither poetry nor joy."

"A new order founded on no freedom."

Out of range of his wife's vision, Indigo's father nods in agreement.

"Stop talking rubbish! If not for my position, that

kind of prattle would land you down the Hatch and in the Root System. Doesn't that frighten you?"

"No, because I don't believe in them," says Indigo. "It's just made up to scare everybody."

"Well, if you don't change your ways and improve your horrid score, you will find out for yourself!"

"My dear Winnie, you simply must calm down. After all, it is only a pretest. With young Thistle tutoring her, she's bound to do better."

"Stop making excuses for them both! Or those old clubs can go back into the cellar where they belong."

"Yes, dear, quite right. No excuses." Her husband clears his throat. "Indigo, as you know, Dale Law School is the very institution from which your mother and I graduated."

"I know, I know, and you both had perfect scores."

"Precisely. Now it is our wish."

"Winston!"

"Sorry, dear, wrong word—as Priggs we do not wish. Indigo, we require you to attend Dale in the fall. Granted as members of the first family, we do have some privilege and can, well, make some adjustments. However, you will have to do better than a score of four."

"But, Pop, I'm just not interested in law."

"Indigo, what else could you possibly want to do with your life?"

"I'd like to study clouds and wind and watch storms

rolling in over the Nethermead."

"Nonsense!" cries her mother. "Certainly, you can glance up at the sky now and again as a hobby, but weather simply is not a career."

Indigo crosses her arms and stares at her mother through narrowed eyes. "But I don't want to be a lawyer."

"What you want is quite beside the point. As governor and your mother, I remind you that with privilege comes responsibility."

"Privilege to do what? To be whatever you tell me to be, think whatever you tell me to think."

Indigo's father sets down the polished pebble then positions his hands and feet to putt.

"Cease your subversive chatter immediately. I may be governor, but I can't protect you from your own willful nature forever."

"I'm willful? What about you telling everybody what to do all the time, including Pop?"

Winston's perfectly lined-up shot hits the wall, the pebble shooting across the floor and bouncing off the governor's slipper. She glowers at her husband.

"Now, Indigo. Your mother does not control me. Completely."

"Winston!"

"What she, I mean we, are asking you to do is quite simple, just learn the laws."

"But, Pop, to spend all day studying 1,999 of them?

There's no time left to think about anything else!"

"There is nothing else!" shouts the governor, pounding the desk with her fist.

"I don't understand them. There's too many. It's too complicated!"

Winston sets aside his club and crosses the room to put his arm around Indigo's shoulder. "At this stage you don't need to understand them. You need only to recite them to get into Dale. And later, after you've studied all the laws of the colonies around the Lullwater, you will learn to manipulate them in the service of the New Order."

"I told you I can't."

"But you used to be such a good student."

"I used to like school, Pop. My nature class was awesome, remember that project you helped me make?"

"Yes, we snuck out that night to gather moss and leaves by the banks of the Lullwater for your diorama of a forest woodland."

"Silence, the two of you. Indigo, you are no longer a little Prigg, and the time has come to put aside those childish studies of nature for a more serious pursuit. The law. And remember—your score must reflect our position as the first family."

"But I don't care, I don't even want to be in the first family if all it means is studying dumb laws and living a useless, boring life!"

"Enough!" cries the governor. "You know that according to our almost last law, as long as they obey, all Priggs will be protected by the New Order, or else!"

"Or else what?"

"Or else that Prigg will be banished. Is that what you want? To be pushed from the uppermost branch? And even if you survive the fall, to be exiled, to live the life of an outlaw stealing sips of nectar from flower to flower in fear of being attacked by a gang of water rats or one of Them with their Beasts?"

"I'm not afraid of Them."

"Well, you should be, Indigo. They put up the Iron Bars, and it's Them that must be feared. Didn't you hear the security report this morning?"

"I was there."

"But clearly you weren't listening to Chief Justice Bitterroot. Now that we're on Alert Level 3, Eon has been patrolling the Lullwater around the clock."

"That old snapping turtle? He can barely move. Let me patrol. I'd make a mad good spy!"

"Mad good?" Her mother looks to her husband who, never having heard the phrase before, can only shrug.

"If either of you ever stuck your head outside this rotting old tree trunk, you'd know it's like excellent."

"Stop talking nonsense, Indigo. What will it take for you to comprehend this clear and present danger? Just an hour ago, Bizby reported the direction and proximity of another Beast barking up into our branches. Do you have any idea how quickly one would gobble up a Prigg foolish enough to step outside?"

"Maybe that would be better than being bored to death by all these useless laws."

"Indigo. We only want what's best for you. So please, while your mother and I are away, be on your best behavior and listen to Justice Bitterroot."

"Pop, really? You're leaving him in charge? But he's even worse than mom!"

"Then perhaps he will have more success getting you to think like a member of this family."

Indigo notices the woven satchels that Martine is setting on the sill where two swallows with long, forked tail feathers perch. "Careful with those clubs," Winston warns the mantis who places the handle of his golf bag in the bird's short, wide beak.

"Where are you going?"

"New Hobb, the colony on the other side of the Lullwater where your father and I will be attending a dinner party, I mean ceremony, in honor of our arrival. Tomorrow is the graduation at Dale where the duke's daughter will deliver the valedictorian speech. Her name is Sage, and we plan on engaging her to work with you throughout the summer."

"No way," groans Indigo. "Not summer school."

"From dawn to dusk. Come, Winston."

"But this is not fair!"

"Not fair? I'll tell you what's not fair. A four is not

fair. In fact, it's an unforgivable way to repay me after all I have sacrificed to protect you and Thistle!"

"Protect us? From what?"

The governor's face pales to a dull shade of blue as she looks toward her husband. She knows that having given into emotion, she has let down her guard—a potentially dire mistake for any politician. Meanwhile Winston in his own well-intentioned, fumbling way quickly comes to her aid.

"What your mother means, Indigo, is that there are, well, several family secrets."

"Winston!"

"I am not saying what they are. I just mean to say, that some things are best left within the family. Matters of birth and such."

"Whose birth?" asks Indigo.

The governor pinches the bridge of her nose. "Winston, just be quiet."

"You said it yourself, Mother. I'm not a little Prigg anymore. If it's about my birth, I have a right to know."

"It doesn't concern you, it concerns your brother." No sooner has the governor uttered the word brother than she cringes at the magnitude of her mistake. "I meant tutor."

"But you said brother. Are you saying Thistle is my brother?"

In the void created by the governor's silence, Indigo hears a loud and reverberating yes—yes that she is not a lonely only child. But that Thistle is her brother, and since they share the same birthday, even better they are twins. After a moment, her mother shakes her head and motions toward a nearby pitcher. "Winston, pour me some lavender."

Obediently he does so, not daring to interject another word for fear of spilling any deeper or darker family secret. He pours the fragrant nectar into a dried cranberry cup and places the calming ale into his wife's trembling hands that he braces with his own as she drinks.

Meanwhile Indigo jumps onto the mushroom sofa and bounces with each exalted word. "I... knew... it... I... knew... it!" Twisting and turning with each bounce, she misses the cushions and lands on the ground at her parents' feet. "I've known it all along—all this nonsense about being blue and not being blue. It's all made up. Thistle and I are the same."

"In a manner of speaking, yes, you are."

"But Pop said secrets. Now that's a good one for starters, but what other secrets haven't you told me?"

"There is at least one other that concerns your tutor," the governor replies.

"You mean my brother."

"Oh well, yes, your brother."

"I'm listening."

"It's a bit more complicated and will take more time than we now have to explain."

23

"You're just trying to wiggle out of this. Why don't you just come clean?"

Her father smiles with admiration. "See, my dear, Indigo does have all the makings of a first-rate lawyer. Just look at how she bullies and badgers—until you find that you are quite beside yourself."

"Winston, be quiet!"

Her husband gestures with his fingertips as if he is zipping shut his violet lips and tossing away an imaginary key. Turning to Indigo, the governor arches her eyebrows. "For once your father is right, Indigo—you win. How about you and I negotiate a deal?"

"What terms do you propose?"

"When I return from Dale, we will sit down and I will give you a full disclosure of this other secret."

"But Pop said several secrets."

The governor glares at her husband. "A full disclosure of several family secrets—but there is one condition."

"Let's hear it."

"While we are away, you must study harder and earn a better grade, a much better grade, a grade more in the vicinity of a 1600."

"Deal." Indigo extends her hand to the governor. "Now remember, verbal agreements are binding. Pop's our witness."

"Yes, Indigo. I will of course keep my word—and you will keep yours." She looks toward the sill where the swallows fully packed are ready to depart. "Where's Bizby? I need him to summon the chief justice."

"Bizby, my dear, seems to have already left for the Nethermead."

"What's happening to this administration? Doesn't anyone follow my orders?"

With bowed head Bitterroot enters. "I am here, Governor."

"How long have you been out there?"

"I just arrived from my chamber," the chief justice lies.

The governor rises. Regaining her composure, she adjusts her Queen Anne's lace collar and air of authority. "As you know, the first husband and I are attending the Dale graduation. Be sure that when we return, you can report better results than a four."

"Yes, Governor, better results."

"Good. In my absence, Chief Justice, I am leaving you in charge. Do whatever must be done!"

"Yes, Governor, whatever must be done."

"Then let us go, Winston. We must make it to New Hobb before the storm." Martine lifts the governor between his strong raptorial forelegs onto the swallow's steely blue back where she grabs hold of the short feathers on the nape of its neck. With considerably more effort, the mantis helps her husband board the other bird. Then in swift, graceful flight, the pair of barn swallows dips and dives into the cool evening air as they take off over the Lullwater.

"Be good, Indigo!" calls her father, the illegal joyfulness in his voice, betraying how happy he is to be leaving the New Order if only for a few days.

"Why bother," mutters Indigo who climbs from the governor's desk onto the edge of the knothole where she watches them disappear into the sky that has grown moody and gray.

CHAPTER THREE

With widespread arms Indigo leaps onto the sofa and dashes about the chamber, imagining she is taking flight over the Nethermead, dodging kites and racing pigeons. Bitterroot claps his hands loudly. "Cease that illegal flapping immediately!"

"I'm just chilling."

"Chilling?"

"You know, fooling around."

"I see. In other words making a fool of yourself."

"No, Bitterroot, I'm playing."

"Which is in violation of Law 776."

"Whatever." Indigo cartwheels across the hardwood floor. "In the Upper Office, I can do what I like. My mother lets me."

"As your mother is no longer here, you must now comply with my orders."

"Says who?"

"Says I."

"Face it, Bitterroot, nobody takes you very seriously." With ease Indigo does a backflip. "Not to hurt your feelings, but you really are something of a joke."

"In the governor's absence, I am in charge of the New Order, and I will be obeyed!"

"Yeah, right."

"Mantis, detain her."

From the ceiling Martine flies down and faces Bitterroot whose eyes bulge with anger at this lowly servant of the New Order who dares to hiss and fan out its wings.

"You will do as I say, mantis, or you will find yourself in the Root System for your refusal to carry out orders." Defiantly the mantis turns his head 90 degrees to the left and then to the right before narrowing his eyes on the chief justice. "Do you dare to threaten me, insect?" The mantis raises and parts his raptorial forelegs then sways gently like a leaf while his calm gaze conveys danger. "Security!"

The harsh clatter of chains dragged through the corridors grows louder with the SF2's approach. Indigo steps closer to Martine, who keeps his spiked forelegs raised and stands ready to fight. Indigo feels a wave of moist heat as two assassin bugs appear in the doorway. Their foul, salivating breath fills the chamber. Like two menacing tanks, they stand three times the size of any Prigg. Each aims its poison proboscis—one at Indigo, the other at Martine.

"Now perhaps, Indigo, you'll believe in the Root System as these assassin bugs are trained members of Security Force 2, its elite armed guards."

"They don't look so elite to me!"

"Perhaps you'd like to feel their sucking mouthparts pierce and paralyze with their painful poison."

"You can't do this."

"I am only following the governor's order to do whatever must be done."

"That's not what she meant!"

"Well, the governor is no longer here to say what she meant, is she? You are under arrest."

"On what grounds?"

"For leaving the elm without authorization."

"You have no proof!"

"Actually," replies Bitterroot whose predatory eyes

narrow. "I was outside the governor's office when your father confessed to sneaking outside with you by night."

"Lots of Priggs go outside."

"Yes, after their application has been approved and they receive their papers, legally."

"But that takes months, and I needed moss for my project."

"So, Indigo, you do admit to unlawful leaving."

"What if I did? It's no big deal. Maximum punishment, thirty hours of community service."

"I also see that you understand more of the law than your abysmal test scores suggest. Perhaps you've been failing your pretests on purpose."

"Perhaps I don't want to go to law school. Perhaps I don't want to be anything that in any way resembles you."

"An interesting admission, Indigo. Tell me more. What else do you know?"

"I know I've done nothing wrong!"

"I disagree, falsifying test scores by pretending you know less than you do is a very serious offense in the New Order—punishable by solitary confinement in the Root System. Unless of course, you are willing to testify against the mantis."

"Never! Martine is only doing his job defending a member of the first family."

"Being a member of the first family is not going to save you this time. Martine is in direct defiance of Law

666, refusal to carry out orders, and will be crushed and disposed of. Your only hope to save yourself is to disavow your alliance to this miscreant insect."

"Never."

Bitterroot grabs the last link of the iron chain that runs out door and down the long corridor and hand over hand drags it into the Upper Office with a deafening clatter. His claws grip Indigo's wrist as he clamps on the manacle. "Take them away!"

Indigo rises in defiance and rattles the chain with all her force and fury.

"No way. No how. Not now. Not ever!"

"Really?" replies Bitterroot calmly. "Pierce her."

The SF2 agent lashes its pincer toward the skin of her slender leg. But as quickly as she jumps back, Martine lunges forward and spews a brown and foul-smelling liquid in the face of the assassin bug.

"Yes, Martine!" shouts Indigo triumphantly. However, this fleeting sense of victory is instantly burst when the second agent shoots out its pincer and pierces Martine's abdomen. The mantis falls heavily to the ground as the poison courses quickly through his body. Tripping over the web of chains, Indigo struggles to reach her wounded friend. "What have they done to you?"

"Very little compared to what you will suffer in the Root System." Bitterroot yanks Indigo to her feet then kicks the poisoned mantis. His mouth drawn into a slit, he exposes the bottom row of his small, sharp teeth. With a leering smile, he delivers his order. "Dispose of the body."

One agent moves toward the wounded mantis that twitches on the ground. Indigo's lungs resound with rage. She has always hated Bitterroot for his arrogance, his ignorance, his pomposity, but now she hates him for his cruelty and the casual pleasure he takes in inflicting pain. Indigo struggles to reach Martine as one agent of the SF2 drags him away. Indigo flails her body left and right, kicking and screaming, as the other agent drags her down the subterranean passageways—where instead of smooth polished floors, the dry wood is rough and splintered and tears the skin of her bare and bloodied feet.

"Halt."

Indigo stumbles and trips over rough-hewn planks, secured to the ground by a rusted bolt.

Rancid vapors seep from a crack between the splintering boards. She covers her face, but still the fumes burn her eyes and nostrils. Bitterroot laughs. Her fury reignites and flames in her chest, her lungs blasting a volley of curses at her captor.

"No one can hear you, and even if someone did, no one can help you now that I am the law. Put her down the Hatch. I'm due to address the Priggs in the courtroom."

The bolt is encrusted with grit and rust, and it takes

the full strength of the agent to force it back. Then on screeching hinges, it lifts the rotting cover to release an even more putrid stench of dirt and decay.

A squadron of gnats, each as big as Indigo's clenched fist, swarms upward and circles her head with a deafening buzz while a legion of white larvae squirms along the portal's edge. On the underside of the Hatch, she sees the woodworms that sensing the warmth of skin inch forward to feast on the blood from her wounded feet.

"Unlink the chain and prepare to push." The SF2 agent positions itself behind Indigo. "Push."

Indigo struggles to hold herself back, but the ground gives way to empty space and she drops. When she opens her mouth to scream, there is no sound. In silence she falls with the long chain unfurling about her—farther and farther, both fearing that she will hit bottom while equally terrified that she will be doomed to descend in this darkness forever.

With the rapid descent and increasing air pressure, painfully her ears pop. Then the sound of the steel links of the long chain rings off the ground and warns her that she is about to crash. Instinctively, she reaches out as if diving into water instead of air. When she hits the gnarly floor of the Root System, the force snaps the shackle from her wrist. Slowly she sits up, dashed by the fall and the swift events that have led to this imprisonment. She listens to the distant creaking of the Hatch being shut as it cuts off the last dim light from above.

Never has Indigo imagined that darkness could be so thick, so impenetrable. Straining her eyes, staring into the void, she tries to make out an edge or a form. Tense and alert, she listens for the drone of a passing gnat or a trickle of water, but there is no sound, no sight in this prison—sinewy cells that have been cut deep into the roots.

The natural inclination in such darkness is to remain still—alert for a flicker of light, afraid that a movement left or right will put you in some grave and unseen danger. Perhaps you are sitting on the edge of an abyss, or only inches away from a coiled and venomous creature ready to strike. All these thoughts pass through Indigo's mind as she crouches on the cold ground with her arms wrapped around her bruised and battered legs.

In this underground cell with no trace of time passing, hours blur in a haze of unknowing. Will she ever eat again, will there ever be a glimpse of light or a breath of sweet grassy air blowing over the Nethermead? To even think of her wounded friend makes her body clench with pain and foreboding. If Indigo is to survive the torment of this isolation, she must now push that thought aside, allowing herself only to imagine the comfort of resting her cheek against Martine's thorax and feeling the flow of his hemolymph and the strength of his quiet, fierce loyalty.

"Believe. I must believe," she utters in the unwavering

darkness. Inhaling deeply, Indigo is grateful for the smell of mulch and earth for she knows that the power of Nature and her own love of freedom, its most powerful expression, will ultimately trump Bitterroot's tyranny.

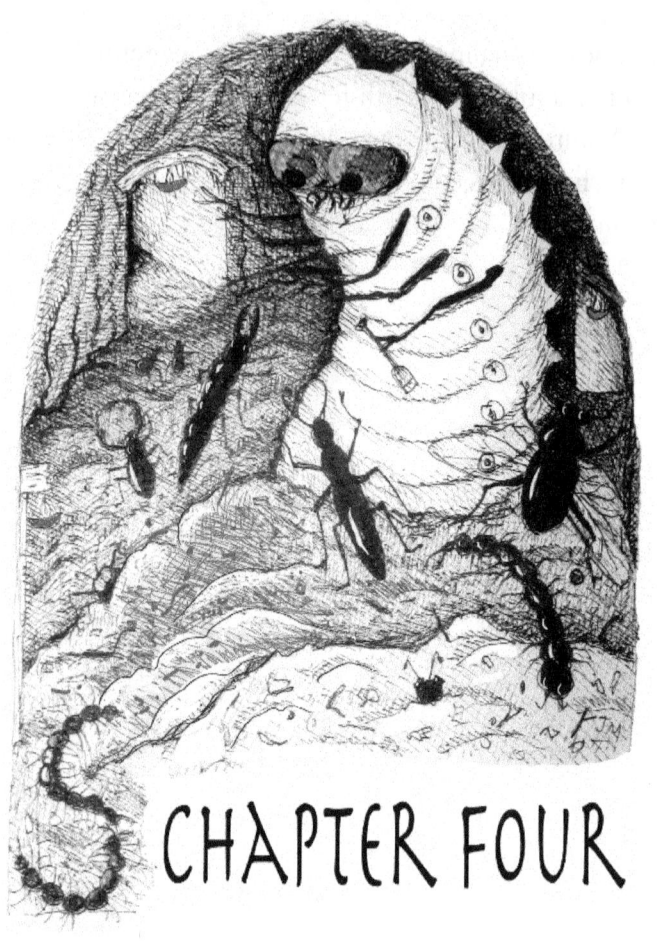

CHAPTER FOUR

Shuffling down the corridor, Thistle makes his way to his mossy niche where he sets his law books on his only shelf. "A four? Really?" he murmurs to himself. "And this is just the beginning. First, it's the compost heap, then banishment. And then what? Alone on the Nethermead—I'll be eaten alive if I'm not stomped to death first." Giving his beloved books a final pat, he makes his way down the long and twisting corridors to the cellar where he has been reassigned to work on the compost heap.

An earthy aroma of rotting leaves and kitchen scraps grows stronger as he approaches. The smell gives him a wave of nausea. He pinches his nose and blinks into the dank area where the compost, a grey brown heap of rotting matter, appears to heave and twitch as if it is alive. His eyes slowly adjust until he can now make out the shape of rove beetles, ground beetles and feather winged beetles, turning and aerating the grit and particles. The foreman, a stout whitish grub with a brownish head and six squirming legs, rises from the mound.

"Halt, who goes there?"

Thistle stands amazed to hear the hearty voice arise from the grub—as strange to him as if a flower or blade of grass has addressed him.

"Well, speak up. What's yer business here on the heap."

"Sorry, sir, it's just that I've never, well, never heard an insect speak."

"Every squeaking, squawking, squirming thing can speak—I'm just the rare bug understands 'em all."

"But I understand you. And I'm a Prigg."

"Well, y'don't look like any Prigg I ever seen."

"I... I'm different."

"Well, then there's your answer. The Priggs see

37

themselves as better. T'their way of thinking they're above Nature herself. Fools all. That'll be their undoing. You on the other hand, seem t'be a more sensible lad. Leastwise, that's what I make of it. What're y'here for?"

"I've been reassigned, sir."

"To the compost heap? That's grub work."

Thistle bows his head. "You see, sir, I failed at my other job."

"No such thing as failure, lad, just Nature taking her course. And if she can't get there this way, she'll go another."

"I'm not sure I understand, sir."

"Maybe not now, but you will. And lose the sir. Down here on the heap, beetle, slug, Prigg—we're all the same. Slinging compost, waiting on the next meal—no matter—which makes you one of us, don't it? Here's your shovel," he says, handing him the tool. "Grit's a bit soggy today, so put some muscle into it. Though you don't look like you ever did much of a day's work."

"I am, I mean I was, a tutor for Indigo, a member of the first family."

"Indigo? Now there's a chatty Prigg."

"You know Indigo?"

"Who in this elm don't? Why, you'll find that blue-blood out and about, here and there, chittering away with any bug, bird or four-legged thing that'll listen."

"Yes, that's Indigo alright."

"So, it was the governor sent you to the Heap."

"No, sir. I was sent by Justice Bitterroot."

"Bitterroot? That bloated son of an undigested piece of meat. The earth ought to puke him and his bad lot up and be done with it."

"But, sir, it's illegal to utter an insult of a chief justice."

"Maybe up there in the chambers, but down here on the heap? We thinks what we please, and we says what we thinks."

Thistle looks about fearfully, his cheeks churning with a rich and throbbing shade of pumpkin pulp.

"Never show them that, my boy."

"What, sir?"

"Fear—they feeds on it."

"Who, sir?"

"Them. The blue bloods—they feed on fear like a dung beetle on dung. Bitterroot and his kind. Gone and turned this tree into a prison is what they did—got it so that nobody but them's got a right to come and go and tend their own business."

"But there is only one business. The business of the New Order—isn't that so, sir?"

"So says them. One business and one business only, to fatten their bellies and their purses. But truth t'tell, every egg and larva's born to be itself and tend to its own business. That's the law."

"But, sir, I've memorized all the laws, and surely that's not one of them."

"Then look deeper, lad, not in your books, but look

deeper inside yourself—it's the law that governs us all from inside out—every creeping, crawling, upright and wrongdoing thing on earth. Why, even the heap here lives and breathes by it."

"And what is that, sir?"

"It's the Law of Nature."

"But no law is above the laws of the New Order—and to even think so is a criminal offense."

"Indeed, Thistle." A noxious voice wafts into the cellar and settles on the compost heap where the startled beetles, alert to danger, cease working and stand still. Bitterroot enters the area, followed by both agents of the SF2. "To say any law is higher is a grave offense. As is the dissemination of false truths."

"The truth's the truth, y'knave, and only them that's grown so fat, they can't hear their own heartbeat deny it."

Bitterroot stabs the air. "Seize him."

"What's the charge?" asks the foreman unfazed.

"I need none. By order of the governor, I am empowered to do whatever must be done." He turns toward the agent. "Dispose of this renegade."

The grub stretches upward and inhales deeply through the spiracles that dot his body. When he stands erect, he towers over the chief justice as he raises his six legs and cries. "Brothers and sisters, arise!"

From the heap of crumbling compost, emerge a legion of larvae, all descendants of the same female beetle who laid her eggs in this dark recess of the roots. They turn toward the foreman who commands, "Follow me to live free without fear!"

Crawling around Bitterroot and his agents, they take up the cry. "Live free without fear."

"Dispose of them all!" shouts Bitterroot. "Poison and pulverize them."

The SF2 point their proboscises in one direction and then another, but the swarming larvae are too many.

"To the Nethermead," the foreman commands his countless siblings who squirm past the outnumbered agents. Abandoning the compost heap, the other beetles follow, some flying while others skitter outside to find soil and substrate beyond the rotting tree trunk.

"They won't last long beyond the New Order. Death to the traitors. You, Thistle, report to the courtroom! All Priggs have been ordered to assemble."

Obediently, Thistle shuffles from the humid cellar to join the coiling line of Priggs who with eyes downcast climb the spiraling staircase. No one speaks. There is only the muffled sound of their steps and the rustle of the leaves of their undergarments while they file into the courtroom and silently seat themselves in the pews.

With much huffing Bitterroot pushes aside two Priggs, giving each a quick clout on the head, moving toward the front of the courtroom where he climbs to his place behind the judge's bench. From this height he forces his audience to strain their necks to look upward as he speaks.

"Be seated."

In one wave of motion all the Priggs sit—their faces a glistening sea of equatorial aqua to deepest night sky blue. All but one whose face glows like a lone dandelion in a field. However, even Thistle bears their look of trouble and confusion, staring mesmerized at the unblinking eyes of the chief justice who glowers down at them.

"Priggs, you are in grave danger."

His words strike every Prigg like a slap in the face. Stunned, they listen with the intensity of prisoners on the verge of sentencing.

"Long have I warned that They and their Beasts are drawing near. However, today was the day, that inevitable day, that one of our own was taken."

All Priggs gulp a breath as if with one lung.

"Yes, the pride of the New Order, a brilliant student on the verge of an illustrious career in law." He pauses to glare down at his audience to heighten the terror of the message he is about to impart. "Taken, tortured, trampled under their monstrous feet, pulverized between the razor-sharp teeth of one of their Beasts to be digested in the hot acids of its stomach—we can only imagine."

With another pause he allows their tainted minds to conjure terrifying scenes of gore and violence. "Taken, tortured, trampled by Them—but driven from the elm by an enemy from within."

The Priggs scan the room and attempt to detect who is the victim missing from their ranks and who is the enemy. "This crime was conceived and committed from within these chambers. It was perpetrated against a member of our own first family."

Again there is a communal gasp. Bitterroot watches a ripple of terror cross their faces. "And if the governor's own child can be taken, tortured, trampled—who among us is safe?"

Thistle's heart beats so rapidly that he stands and clutches his chest. It is then that all eyes like arrows shoot across the room from every direction, piercing him with accusations before he has even been accused.

"A crime committed by the very Prigg the governor entrusted to tutor Indigo. The very Prigg who stands trembling before you."

"But I would never hurt Indigo. Besides, we were together in the law chamber all afternoon."

"Indeed, you were the last to see her—and to lure her outside and onto a treacherous limb. All this was seen and reported to me by Bizby."

"But that's not how it was at all. I was trying to get Indigo to come back inside. Besides, why would I hurt her? Indigo is my student." Thistle hesitates before murmuring, "and my friend."

"Student, perhaps, but you are more fiend than friend."

43

"But I have no reason to harm her."

"In fact, there is a very probable cause." All eyes shift from Bitterroot to Thistle whose face is now fully drained of color. "Would you say you are a capable student of the law, Thistle?"

"Yes, but I don't see how...?"

"Yes or no, Prigg. Have you not mastered all the laws of the New Order?"

"Yes."

"And being so excellent a student, were you not assigned by the governor to tutor Indigo."

"Yes, I was."

"And is it not your own dream to attend Dale to study law?"

"Yes, it is." Thistle whispers, "very much,"

"The very institution to which Indigo would have been admitted in the fall."

"Only if she passed the entrance exam."

"Indeed. And what score did she receive on the pretest?"

Thistle hesitates and then responds with his eyes still downcast. "Four."

"Four, ladies and gentlemen. A brilliant student of law tutors a member of the first family, and rather than instruct, he mis-educates."

"That's not true. I did my best."

"Silence. You are in enough trouble."

"But I didn't do anything."

"You did nothing to prevent the fatal fall that you premeditated."

"I didn't, I swear I didn't."

"You were jealous of Indigo, weren't you? Admit it, you were so jealous that you sabotaged her studies so that she would fail the exam."

"That's not true, I tried my best to teach her."

"Yes, to teach her only four out of the 1,999 laws that you know by heart. And yet you knew that her parents, both esteemed graduates of that institution, could use their connections to get her admitted to Dale in the fall." Bitterroot stands silently observing the nodding Priggs who are following his twisted logic. "And so driven by jealousy, you shoved her out onto the limb to either be impaled on the spikes of the Iron Bars or fall into the hands of the enemy and the jaws of their Beasts."

"But that's not how it happened at all!" protests Thistle whose high-pitched pleas are smothered by the maniacal shouts of the mob. "Yes, she fell, but I sent for Martine to rescue her. Ask the mantis. He'll tell you the truth."

"The dead can speak no truth."

The Priggs are aghast at this horrible revelation that Martine, beloved by all, is dead. They suck in and hold one breath before letting out cries of disbelief and indignation. Equally shocked, Thistle murmurs, "Martine dead, but how?"

"Heroically trying to save your victim. It wasn't

enough that by luring Indigo out onto that limb you sentenced her to certain death, but then you summoned the mantis. There from the knothole in the law library, you sent it directly into the path of a ravenous squirrel to be devoured."

"But that's not true!"

"Do not deny it. Bizby was entering the knothole at that precise moment. Being the eyes of the New Order, he watched aghast at your treachery. Based on Bizby's sworn testimony, I charge you with two counts of murder. How do you plead, Thistle? Or shall I call you traitor?"

Taking up the taunt, all Priggs raise their fists and chant. "Traitor, traitor, traitor."

"Innocent, I am innocent," murmurs the prisoner who knows that no matter how loud he might shout, his truth will be drowned out by the crashing waves of their ignorance and hatred.

"Order in the court. Before I instruct you to reach a verdict in this case. There is a secret, an insidious secret that must finally be brought to light."

Now the attention of the crowd has been recaptured and silence enshrouds the room. "It is a secret concealed by the governor. It is a secret that all in her family fear your knowing." Bitterroot pauses as the Priggs pant—drooling and ravenous for Bitterroot's revelation. "Since the founding of the New Order of the World, only blue bloods have governed. Yet she has lied about her own family's bloodline, a bloodline that is tainted."

"That's a lie," retorts Thistle who for the first time in his life dares to challenge the chief justice. "You have no proof!"

"No proof? You, Thistle, are the proof." Then addressing the courtroom, he declares, "The proof that is as undeniable as the non-blue blood that runs through your veins. For you, Thistle, are the governor's own son!"

Now a shock wave of confusion and indignation convulses the courtroom as their doubts and murmurings sweep across the room—son, Thistle? No, impossible, he has no blue blood, not a drop.

"Not a drop, indeed. And yet the twin of Indigo, born to the same mother, the former governor who with her husband concealed this hideous lie—that the first family is not of true-blue blood!"

No one in the room stands more shocked, more torn to pieces by this secret than Thistle. All his life, he has been shunned by all except Indigo—who now has been revealed to be his twin. On one hand, his heart aches with a sad joy that they are one. On the other, his heart breaks at the rejection of his own parents.

So painful is this contradiction that for a moment Thistle tries to deny it. Why he reasons, after all the lies that have been spewed throughout this trial, why should he believe Bitterroot's words now?

Simply and profoundly because Thistle's own heart is throbbing with their truth.

"Yet, there is a second secret. The governor spoke of it before her departure." Bitterroot turns toward Thistle. "A second secret that I believe you too harbor in your discolored heart."

Thistle's eyes widen for indeed this secret he has had to conceal his whole life.

"However, being merciful, I will offer you, traitor, a chance to perhaps save yourself from certain death. For as you know, if you are found guilty of all charges, you will by the laws of the New Order of the World be sentenced to die. Save yourself and reveal it now."

Thistle looks toward the SF2 agents that aim their weapons at him. He stands straighter now and clenches his fists that turn scarlet red, not in fear but in fury. He will claim this truth as his own—he will reveal it with an honesty so brutal, he will destroy their lies with his truth.

In his deepest being Thistle has always known that this moment would come, the moment when he would be called upon to disrobe and stand naked before all the Priggs to reveal his secret. But never did he imagine that he would do so with pride and defiance.

Thistle unknots the sash of his tunic then reaches down and clasps its hem. Pulling the folds of its fabric over his head, he tosses it into the crowd. He stands before them, steady on his long and skinny tangerine legs, as the leaves of his breeches rustle in the foul breath of the bullying mob.

Around his chest is wound a long and slender cloth that slowly he unwraps as he twirls before their gawking eyes until finally undone, the cobweb cloth falls to his feet. Now standing before them with his bare back exposed, Thistle reveals to their horror the second secret—two wings—too tiny and shriveled from disuse to carry him beyond the chaotic cries of their hatred but wings nonetheless that freed from their harness, flutter meekly with a gentle grace.

"These are my truth!"

Currents of disgust run through the crowd as mothers cover their children's eyes and others rise, yelling taunts and threats at the exposed Sprite.

"There can be only one verdict in this case," Bitterroot cries out.

"Guilty, guilty, guilty," they chant with narrow eyes and grimacing faces.

"And one punishment!" Bitterroot snaps his fingers at the agents who stand in the doorway. "Take it away!"

Thistle throbs with a deep, undying crimson—a shade of red which will streak the sky at sunset for as long as the atmosphere like a bloody bandage still wraps around the earth.

One hundred hands push and shove one another out of the courtroom and up the spiraling stairs. They lash the prisoner with their curses, despising him more intensely with each step, as they drive out the condemned Sprite onto the uppermost limb.

Watching from inside the elm, the chief justice raises his foreleg to silence the Priggs. He then points toward the prisoner and orders the SF2.

"Push!"

The assassin beetles skitter from the knothole toward Thistle to deliver the fatal shove. But nimbly he outpaces them as he crawls toward the tip of the branch. There Thistle rises. He feels the crisp night air that blows through the leaves of his breeches and caresses the feathers of his tiny useless wings. Although he knows they cannot carry him to safety, instinctively he leaps.

Plummeting toward the earth like a plucked acorn, he turns his eyes upward to behold the great arc of the star-studded sky. Against the buttery light of a gibbous moon, he sees the silhouette of a bat that is swooping toward him. With the perfect timing of Nature, Thistle lands between the flapping wings that carry him over the treetops.

CHAPTER FIVE

Old Order of the World 1566

The River Avon winds through the town of Stratford, its banks flourishing with overhanging trees and clumps of wildflowers. The air resounds with twittering and trills, the rustling of leaves and water running over rocks. From the branch of a willow, a kingfisher eyes the silvery form of small carp that suns itself near the surface and warms its back. In a flash the bright blue and rust colored bird darts down to pierce the water to nab the fish and fly off with its catch still flapping in its beak. Meanwhile two winged-creatures flit among a cluster of white-flowered teasels as they zigzag between the long and prickly stems until one of their wings gets caught and the other laughs.

"I win!"

"Tis not fair, Cobweb."

"Why, Peaseblossom, because thou hath lost?"

"No, because thou always wins," whines the Sprite that yanks its wing free from the flower.

"Look there's, Zinnia! Maybe she will play."

"Oh, Cobweb, go not near, for she is with a mortal."

"Let's spy on her to tell the other Sprites what business Zinnia has with one of them."

"Be wary, there are two."

"Two? The other is but a belching baby, barely in breeches. I fear not babies."

"Hush, they draw near."

From beneath the jagged edge of a leaf, they watch the woman who wears a blue bodice and a red skirt that billows in the breeze while she hurries along to keep up with the boy. She carries in her hand a wooden paddle until finding a sunny spot in the green grass, she spreads her shawl.

"What's that the female carries?"

"A weapon."

"Foolish Zinnia is too close, too close," squeals
Peaseblossom. *"We must warn her."*

The woman sits with her face toward the sun while
her son toddles among the wildflowers, laughing happily
when Zinnia swoops by him only to fly out of reach of
his outstretched fingers. He laughs more loudly as two
more Sprites join their game and fly from a nearby
branch to grab hold of Zinnia's arms. They tussle midair
until they pull her down into a patch of purple fox glove.

*"Let go! Let go I say. How dare you interrupt my
play? When I am queen, I'll have thee locked away."*

"Yes, Zinnia, we've heard that threat before!"

"Oh, goodly Queen, forgive us we implore!" Cobweb
bows with mock reverence to Zinnia who struggles to be
released from their grip.

"How dare you assault and then insult me?"

*"We neither wish insult nor harm. But the mortal,
Zinnia, she is armed!"*

*"Armed? With what weapon? She hath no weapon
other than her wit. She is Mary of Arden. And she is
most wondrous bright."*

*"Then why hath she a paddle if not to clobber foolish
Sprites?"*

*"Who's foolish now? They call it a hornbook. On it
are writ' the letters of their language, the very language
that we speak. And she is teaching her son—and me who
sits perched on his shoulder—to master them. There are*

twenty-four and each one has a glorious shape!"

"And so, you waste your morning thus—when you could cruise the sky with us?"

"My time with Mary is well spent. This farmer's daughter must have lived in realms beyond this market town because she tells the most amazing tales that make both me and Will quite wide-eyed with delight."

"Who's Will?"

"Her little boy whose laughter's like the song of nightingales. Me thinks he must be a changeling for his eyes do glimmer with unearthly magic."

"Then we too must meet this Mary of Arden."

"And play with this changeling child."

"And learn the letters."

"No lessons for me," says Cobweb, "but I do like a goodly tale."

Furious, Zinnia tears hers arms from their grip, and with a powerful shove of two hands on Cobweb's chest she pushes him and then Peaseblossom to the ground.

"No, you will not. Mary is my friend and Will my boy. Let you not disturb us by this river again, or else I'll give thee more of this." She glares at them with clenched fists raised and ready to punch.

Stepping back, Peaseblossom whispers. "Come, Cobweb, when she's angry, she is keen and shrewd!"

"Remember when we played with ball and twig? How when she lost, she punched my eye and called me prig."

"Aye, I do. Though she be but little, she is fierce."

"With her I would not choose to battle just to hear this Mary prattle."

Cobweb turns to face the angry Sprite. *"Okay, Zinnia. You stay with your changeling boy while we make mortals into toys."*

"Come, Cobweb, let's fly to the market square, to tip their carts and pull their hair!"

"Yes, Zinnia must study with her betters until in time she grows bored of letters."

"Grow bored of letters? Never! Words will be my power, and I will wield them over all you feckless Sprites."

"Oh, listen how us Sprites she does demean as if already she were Queen."

"Let's fly, the bell doth strike'th ten, 'tis time to play our pranks on men."

While Peasesblossom and Cobweb race to the marketplace in Stratford, Zinnia makes her way through the jagged stems of fox glove. When she hears the babbling of the small boy, she flies to where he sits sobbing in his mother's lap. His crying ceases when the Sprite hovers before him. She kisses her fingertip then places it on his lips that immediately curl upward and part to let loose a chorus of bright laughter.

CHAPTER SIX

Over New Hobb a brisk wind off the Lullwater flaps a newly woven flag. It has been dyed a shade of overripe plum and raised in honor of the arrival of the Priggish governor. Maple leaves have been spread over a flat rock and set with platters of steaming wild delicacies and acorn pitchers of blackberry punch that glisten in the moonlight.

Gliding across the Lullwater, a sleek scull with two long oars like insect legs churning the water propels the duke's daughter toward shore. It is a long, slim vessel that Sage has built from reeds on which she has won many competitions at Dale. With each pull of the oars, the seat on a long smooth track slides toward the bow of the scull then back to the stern. Enjoying the smooth almost effortless ride, the young Hobb feels like she's flying through the cool night air which ruffles the soft brown fur that covers her head and ears, coming to a peak over her brow.

Alongside the boat flies a Luna moth whose pale green wings cast a shadow over the rower. Four false eyes fearfully embellish its wings, warding off any hungry bat along with two long spinning tails, designed by Nature to disrupt a predator's sonar.

Sage speaks to her as she rows. "I don't know about this whole graduation thing, Luna. Okay, I'll do the speech tomorrow, no big deal. But the dinner party tonight? What am I supposed to do, put on a big toothy smile for the governor and her husband?" Sage skillfully maneuvers the scull alongside a flat rock and angles an oar onto it. As the light vessel can be easily flipped, she lifts herself up with care and places one paw onto to the moss-covered mudstone and then the other. Walking along the bank, she stops at a bush where a leafy tunic hangs from a branch. Adorned with fiddlehead ferns, it is in the Priggish style and Sage, forced to wear it for the weekend, has left it here to postpone its imprisonment until the arrival of her father's guests.

"Think about it, Luna. They're Priggs. None of them work. They just make every other living thing do their bidding. It's not right. And what am I supposed to do, just bow and say how do you do, like I'm okay with that?" She pulls the homespun robe over her muscular torso. "Hobbs in clothes, ridiculous," she mutters before making her way toward the buffet table. Here she pauses, entranced by the trays of pastries drizzled with honey, crispy fried dandelion leaves and dumplings plump with delicacies she can only imagine—because Sage is forbidden to eat them.

Shutting her brown eyes and furrowing her leathery brow, she fights the urge to eat, mentally struggling to ignore the aroma of freshly foraged mushrooms grilled to perfection. Physically, however, she cannot stop her stomach from rumbling, nor her hand from creeping toward a particularly fat dumpling, lightly browned and sprinkled with pale seeds that in her mind is softly calling her name.

The wide-winged moth perched on a low branch swoops down to conceal her from the oncoming white-haired Hobb who tugs at his own ill-fitting tunic. Sage looks up. Although her mouth waters and her outstretched fingertips can feel the moist warmth of the dumpling dough, she releases the tasty morsel to turn and smile awkwardly at her approaching father.

"Sage, step away from the table. None of this food is on your diet." Standing beside the stem of a dandelion, the duke reaches up and grabs a jagged leaf, causing a shower of silvery seeds to rain down. He rips off an edge and hands it to his daughter. "Here, eat salad. How much food have you consumed today?"

Before dawn Sage had secretly eaten a wedge of honeycomb that exceeded her daily allotment four times over. "Four leaves," she lies, gnawing at the bitter buttery greens.

Scornfully her father surveys his daughter. "Look at your feet, they're covered in mud. We have guests coming. Don't you have any pride?"

"Dad, I just graduated from Dale with honors. I'm the valedictorian, remember? Don't I get any credit for that?"

"Don't change the subject, Sage. You've got to show more concern for your appearance. And that includes losing some weight before you depart for your summer job."

"Summer job, where?"

"You'll be working for the New Order."

"The Priggish colony? No way ever!"

"You're to be hired to work as a tutor for the first family. And it's merely a first step in my plans for you."

"First step? Maybe I have plans of my own."

As he so often does, the duke mimics Sage's words

in a whiney voice. "Maybe I have plans of my own." Then he shifts back to his usual harsh tone. "The only plans that can concern you are mine. Why do you think I went into hock sending you to Dale in the first place? Besides, a Hobb in service to the New Order of the World will be very advantageous."

"Whoa, hold on there. In service to Priggs? Not me, I'm a freeborn Hobb."

"And it's time you stop thinking like one."

Sage watches her father's thick paw reach for the very dumpling that she had nearly nabbed. While he continues to drone on about social obligations and family honor, he chews it loudly, releasing the mingled aroma of wild scallion and fried acorn. As he lectures, Sage's eyebrows come to life in a way that only her eyebrows can—in a way that is out of her control and which always infuriates her dad.

Before fully swallowing the savory morsel, in one sweeping motion her father grabs and devours a pastry. Sage watches the flurry of yellow crumbs shower down and settle between the shaggy hairs on his feet. "And on top of that, you want me to give you credit for graduating from Dale? If anyone deserves credit, it's me. So yes, you are going to work for the governor this summer. And just maybe their Priggish way of life will whip you into shape."

Inwardly fuming at her father's insults, Sage narrows her eyes and glares. Her right eyebrow rises higher than the other then leans leftward, creating a ridge that resembles a short snake that uncoils between her eyes and pulses with her suppressed rage.

Her father glances up from the platter of mushrooms that he is sniffing. "Cut that out! Their birds are due to land any minute. Do you expect me to introduce you with that grotesque wrinkle on your brow? Don't embarrass me, they're real live Priggs!"

"And we're Hobbs. Get over it. We have paws and big hairy feet."

"Don't call them paws, these are hands. A little leathery perhaps, but hands nonetheless."

"Hobbs work, Priggs don't. They live shut-up inside a half-dead tree and do nothing but pretend that somehow makes them better. And now you want to make a servant out of me, your own daughter? It's intolerable!"

Overhead two barn swallows dip downward with outstretched wings to land in a nearby clearing. The duke hurries to meet their incoming flight, waving as he shouts. "Welcome, Governor! Winston, so good to see you again."

"Good to see you, Duke," shouts back the first husband, who with some effort deboards the bird. "And I must say, I am quite looking forward to a few rounds of golf!"

"In due time, Winston," his wife rebukes him before sliding genteelly to the ground and smoothing out the folds of her travel-rumpled robe. "Oh, and this must be Sage. My how you've grown," she says with her eyes settling on her waistline.

"Yes, I was just speaking to Sage about slimming down a bit before heading off for the New Order."

"Nonsense," interjects Winston. "This young woman is a hale and hearty athlete. I heard how the Dale crew won a very exciting race. Rowing crew takes discipline, skill, physical power, eh, Paige?"

"Paige," Sage mutters under her breath.

"Ah yes, quite true, Winston," chimes in the governor whose high-pitched voice makes Sage's eyebrows rapidly twitch. "It is very prestigious to row crew for Dale. And to graduate as valedictorian. We are quite thrilled at the prospect of you joining us this summer."

"Sage, don't just stand there gaping, go get their bags."

"When you come to us this summer," the governor continues to croon in a false and friendly tone, "your only duty will be to tutor Indigo. All the other labor? Well, we have servants for that."

The duke's lips stretch into a stiff smile. "Won't that be wonderful, Sage?"

"Oh, Duke, wonderful is against New Order of the World Law 947. But graduating at the top of her class, Sage already knows that," responds the governor. Having intended to compliment the Hobb, she is confused when scowling Sage emits a growl as her eyebrows pulse even more furiously. Grabbing the neckline of her Priggish tunic, she grasps the organic fabric between her clawed fingers and tugs with a force that rips it apart. "Oh, my," says the governor. "Is she always quite so volatile?"

"How dare you?" growls her father, shaking a fist at his daughter who storms off. "I'm warning you, Sage, if you leave, don't come back."

"I won't," she shouts as she bounds away on all fours toward the pond. Although muscular and big-boned, Sage is agile and light on her leathery feet and gracefully steps into the scull before centering herself on the sliding seat with her knees to her chest. With both long oars firmly grasped, she pulls back and stretches out her legs then glides forward to execute the next pull, propelling the boat beyond the cries of her outraged father.

Alongside the scull flies Luna with the moonlight softly illuminating its wings. The moth's gentle rhythm along with the forward movement of the boat calms Sage as she feels her own breathing synchronize with the flow of the air and water around her.

Arcing above the Lullwater, the great sky is veiled by a swirling mist that conceals and reveals countless pinpoints of light. Nothing in her classes at Dale has taught her the source of this infinite beauty—but scanning the shore with the sharp vision of a Hobb, she sees a thousand eyes stare back at her: bug eyes, possum eyes, eyes of raccoons, bullfrogs and owls. These she knows, and to them she feels connected, recalling all her tramping, camping, exploring among them. Peacefully Sage continues to row, inhaling the moist night air, lulled by the duet of crickets and cicadas while Luna flies above the bow of the boat.

Suddenly the hairs on her ears spring up. On silent wings a bat swoops down, its talon pinching the pelt at the back of Sage's neck. Its grip, however, is loosened by the unexpected swat of her small, but powerful paw. Alarmed by the tussle, Luna rises to lure away the attacker. The bat aims for the false eyes on the moth's wings and lunges at its prey with open claws. When it misses, Luna flies upward with her tails spinning, throwing its sonar out of whack. Disoriented, the bat swerves and flies away when off its back, a thin and screeching creature falls toward the water. Sage watches it drop into the Lullwater, leaving its imprint on the mill floss. For a moment the night is deadly still—until with a splash and a gasp, a bristly head pops above the surface and emits a gurgling cry for help before being swallowed up again.

Sage rises and steps onto shell of the scull to dive into the dark and inky water, overturning the vessel that floats off with the powerful thrust of her haunches. She swims downward into the murky currents, passing a snapping turtle as large as an ancient submerged island. Eon on watch for the New Order observes the tiny commotion of the mouse-like creature that wraps a foreleg around what appears to be a wilted dandelion as it swims upward. When with a splash it breaks the surface, the slender stem of a body comes to life, sputtering and flailing. Sage keeps its head above water as she scans the Lullwater, but the scull is nowhere in sight.

With her head tilted back and her ears submerged, she keeps a firm hold on the limp creature whose shallow breathing is the only sign that it is still alive. Sage uses her free paw to sweep the water with each powerful kick thrusting them across the Lullwater. Hours pass and still Sage swims, her legs continuing to kick although with decreasing force as her right arm grows numb keeping the creature afloat. But still she keeps stroking the water with her left paw, intent on reaching the far shore.

Sage breathes calmly but is constantly aware that the massive turtle that had been witnessing the rescue might be following, waiting for her to weaken before snapping her in two and gobbling her down—or that a large mouth bass might open wide and suck them both in before grinding them between its rows of sharp teeth. But she also understands the most dangerous predator on the Lullwater is fear, and that to survive she must not surrender to it. Finally, she feels the slope of the earth rise and the depth of the water diminish until she is lying on the grassy shore, her tired limbs sinking into the muddy ground. On her chest the drenched and spindly creature coughs and spits out pond water. It lifts its head, then rolls off her heaving chest and asks in a tremulous voice, "Sir, are you going to eat me now?"

"Am I what? No! Why?"

"Because that's what They do. They take, they torture, they trample. But their Beasts? They just devour you."

"What are talking about? They who?"

"Them. The ones who put up the Iron Bars. Don't you belong to Them?"

"I don't belong to anybody. I'm a Hobb, and I happen to be a vegetarian. And even if I ate other creatures, which I find repulsive, you don't look particularly appetizing. What are you anyway?"

"I'm a Prigg."

"Yeah, right."

"In fact, I am the governor's son." Uttering these words for the first time feels strange, however Thistle's spine straightens, and he stands to face the furry stranger and look directly into her dark eyes.

"Really? Well, I just saw the governor on shore, and you don't exactly look like a blue blood."

"I'm different," replies the creature who stands in his grassy breeches and slowly turns his back toward the Hobb who gasps.

"I know, know," Thistle groans. "They're puny, pathetic, useless."

"No, just the opposite. They're very promising."

Thistle strains his neck, trying to look over his shoulder, spinning in circles to see his wings. "They're still on the small size, but they're kind of, you know, robust and at the same time, fluffy." And as Sage praises Thistle's wings, they grow even fuller and fluffier, and in the creamy moonlight they gently shimmer—peach, pale crimson and blue.

With a will of their own, the wings begin to flap, barely raising Thistle off the ground. At first his amber eyes convey a mix of confusion and pleasure as he hovers but then widen with terror when the wings gain momentum. Flailing his arms, he tries to grab hold of a reed, a wild mustard leaf, a fern—anything to anchor himself, but instead he careens wildly, knocking into a berry bush, nearly dropping into the open jaws of an expectant bullfrog. Then to the frog's disappointment, Thistle's wings suddenly draw him upward to soar alongside a June bug, its loudly buzzing wings distorting his cries for help.

Before the wayward wings can transport Thistle over the Lullwater, he grabs hold of the tip of a branch where he dangles dangerously above the bullfrog that is still eyeing him with interest. But as unexpectedly as his wings swept him away, they sleepily fold in on themselves, leaving Thistle to sway in the breeze far above Sage's head.

"Cool," shouts Sage.

"Cool? I could have been killed. How do I get down

from here?"

"I don't know, they're your wings. I guess you have to learn how to control them. Try giving them an order."

"Wings, I command you to land me back on the ground."

Lazily the wings stretch before tucking themselves back under his shoulders.

"Looks like they don't take orders," observes Sage, whose brow wrinkles with the effort of holding back her laughter. "You could try..."

"Try what?"

"Try not thinking about it."

"How do you think about not thinking about something?"

"It's like when I'm rowing. There's a point when I'm rowing and I'm not thinking about rowing. It's actually quite nice."

"Okay, wings. I'm not thinking about you landing me back on the ground." His wings stir but do not spread.

Suddenly the bullfrog lunges. Its beady eyes and open jaws are now set on Sage who appears as vulnerable and tasty as any tiny rodent. Equally agile, the Hobb snaps a twig from a nearby shrub, instantly arming herself to fight for her life while without thinking, Thistle soars downward to pummel its head with a volley of small, but distracting kicks.

"Take that and that and that!" he shouts at the

unfazed frog. But his battle cry ends abruptly when a chunk of ice crashes down to the ground, and hail begins to fall from lofty, black-bottomed clouds. A bolt of energy cracks a path in the air that closing in on itself creates a rumble of thunder that rocks the earth, warning all creatures to take shelter. Even the predator, a breath away from devouring its prey, dives back into the Lullwater.

Thistle, who has never been outside in a storm, quivers with the shock of the blasts. "It's Them! They've launched another sky attack."

"Nonsense, it's just a storm, but we've got to take cover," shouts Sage whose voice is carried off by the gusts of wind that rattle and shake the reeds and rushes high above their heads. On all fours she bounds toward the bridge that spans the mouth of the Lullwater. "Follow me."

"Follow her," commands Thistle who having gained full control over his wings flies after Sage toward the cavern below the cast iron bridge.

CHAPTER SEVEN

Deep below the surface of the earth, the prisoner grows weak with waiting. Although she fights off sleep, alert to any sound or stirring that might portend either rescue or destruction, wearily her head bobs forward. Several times Indigo jolts herself awake. But even when she dozes off, there is no escape from the gnawing fear of this total isolation—no sight, no sound, no movement. Lowering and raising her eyelids, Indigo faces the same void. Exhausted her body and mind sink into a deep and dreamless sleep, maybe for minutes, maybe for hours— until an incessant rap, tap, tapping disrupts the silence and draws her back to the cold, dark reality of the Root System.

"Martine?" she whispers for a moment having forgotten that her comrade is not there and that she is dangerously alone. Indigo listens. Recognizing the rhythm of the woodpecker, she waits and watches for a pinpoint of light to pierce the darkness. Shreds of sapwood rain down as the hole widens, and a long sharp beak penetrates the trunk, admitting a shaft of moonlight. "Thanks," she calls to the woodpecker who continues to chip away and widen the hole before flying off.

In the narrow beam of light, she now has a dim view of the Root System where overhead, hanging from the silvery strands of a forsaken web, dangles the dried-out body of a dead fly. She crawls toward a downward sloping portal and peers into its inky darkness. When outside a sudden breeze blows through the treetops, a rush of air blows over the hole in the trunk, sounding a low note that reverberates through the hollow elm. Indigo watches as a thread of vapor passes through the hole and like a veil let loose on a windy day unfurls in the air.

Slowly it descends and hovers before her, radiating its own cool light while spinning into a pale and palpitating globe. When Indigo opens her hand, softly it lands, folding in on itself before transforming into a dandelion with countless silvery seeds.

Indigo recalls one morning how after sneaking outside to catch a glimpse of the Nethermead, she studied one of Their children that was playing in the grass just beyond the Iron Bars. It had plucked a dandelion stem and then blew hard on the puff ball, laughing as the seeds flew off in all directions. Imitating the child, Indigo inhales deeply now and with her breath blasts away the airborne seeds that rise and swirl. As the shower ends, she feels a rustling in her hand. Now where the flower had been, there appears a tiny bird whose transparent feathers glow with a pulsating light emitted by its fragile, beating heart.

When the spirit bird flies upward, Indigo rises to follow its flight. But when it reaches the shaft in the floor, it momentarily hovers before darting downward. Fearful of descending to an even more remote dungeon, she crawls back, chirping for the ghost bird to return. Saddened by the silence, Indigo falls back onto the cold ground and lapses into the despair of this total isolation.

Restlessly her mind wanders through the upper chambers, her thoughts leading her to Thistle's niche. There she can always find him on the moss-filled mattress, studying his law books. But in her mind's eye, she finds it empty, and an uneasy feeling tells her that Thistle is in danger. Shaking off despair, Indigo opts for hope, for she must escape to protect her friend and all the Priggs of the New Order from the evil intent of Chief Justice Bitterroot.

The sound of fluttering rises from the hole in the ground. With the bright chirping that follows, she sits up and crawls toward it. But when the pressure of her hands causes the ground to crumble and collapse, Indigo tumbles down the short, steep passageway and descends to the lowest level of the Root System. Hitting bottom, she lands on a pile of hollow twig-like things. Dry and brittle, they scatter and break with a dull clatter.

Without seeing, a voice inside her says—bones.

On hands and knees, she scrambles quickly away and crawls into a niche in the root where she shudders with revulsion and the unbearable cold. Her eyes adjust to the pulsing light emitted by the heartbeats of the phantom bird. More clearly now, she sees the scattered bones and can even make out the skull of the former prisoner who long ago exhaled a final breath in this dank and lonely place.

Momentarily the bird perches on the skull and sings before flying above a hulking, boxlike object. It is taller than it is wide and has a dome-shaped top. When the bird perches on the lid, its incandescent heart reveals a bluish glow and glitter which piques Indigo's natural curiosity and lures her closer. Parting its glassy beak to trill a series of high notes, the little ghost seems pleased to have led the imprisoned Prigg to this discovery.

Indigo walks cautiously around it, examining what appears to be an ancient trunk designed for distant travel. Its framework is covered by a hide of thick, tanned leather, and although its sides are scuffed and dented, it is sturdily reinforced with bands of iron. She runs her fingers over the crystal encrusted lid—the same blue Derbyshire crystals that adorn her father's golf clubs.

When the bird alights and flies around the tomb, a glint of silver catches Indigo's eye. It is a tarnished medallion, still visible beneath a patina of mottled grey and black. She crouches beside the trunk, squints and focuses on the flowering branches etched into the metal that encircle a monogram. Indigo runs her fingertips over the twirling line of letters, making out a Q and Z. Curiosity swells within her chest to see what is inside, but whatever is within has been protected from thieving hands by a heavy, rusted lock. Hesitantly, Indigo reaches out to take hold and rocks it like an old and loose tooth. After one hard tug the hasp, barely attached by a displaced screw, snaps off. With the weighty lock still in its grip, it falls with a thud to the ground.

On her knees, she places her palms under the rim of the blue inlaid lid and pushes upward. Although she grunts with the effort, the lid barely moves.

Then a rattling arises from the nearby pile of bones.

Alert she listens to the tip-tap-tapping, tip-tap-tapping come closer and closer. Then in the sputtering glow that illuminates their path, two skeletal hands skitter like spiders toward her. With a gasp she lets the lid drop, shielding her face, certain that she is about to be attacked for having touched what once had been the last possession of the prisoner who long ago had died here.

"Sorry," she utters. "I was only going to look."

But still the hands approach—tip-tap-tap, tip-tap-tap toward where Indigo crouches. She can feel the light pressure of their boney fingertips as they creep up her arms. Their sharp tips scratch her shoulders, but rather than claw and gouge, the hands reach out to gently clasp her wrists and lower them from her eyes. They then glide toward the top of the trunk where side by side with Indigo's hands, they push it open a crack, releasing a silvery mist that seeps through the opening and dimly illuminates the cell in pale blue light. When together they heave the lid open, the blended sounds of gurgling water and light-hearted laughter rise.

Still uncertain if her curiosity will be welcomed or punished, cautiously Indigo moves back—until both hands extend their index fingers and curl them inward, inviting her to peek. Leaning over the rim and peering inside, she sees a river circling in on itself in a figure eight—lazily it streams east to west and then east again. On its surface dip and dive two tiny, winged creatures no bigger than her thumb, who from the patter Indigo feels

75

in her own chest, she recognizes as her ancestors, the river spirits of Old Elm.

Only once before has she ever been so close to a body of water. That was the night that she snuck out of the tree trunk with her father to collect moss for her nature project. In the moist grass she had kicked off her slippers to run along the spongy bank. There in the moonlight, her bare feet splashing in the cool water, she had felt more alive than she had ever felt in the half-dead elm of the New Order.

Now lured by the rhythm of the crisscrossing currents, Indigo raises a leg over the rim of the trunk and pulls herself up to sit and dangle her wounded feet over the grey-green water. She feels the cool, moist air on her skin, then tips her toes into the brisk cold stream.

For a moment she is blinded by a bolt of light that ignites the Root System—first with light and then with a thunderous explosion. She feels the energy crackle and catch fire in every cell of her body as she falls forward. The distance which a moment before had only been the length of an outstretched arm is now as wide as the Nethermead itself. Free falling past the treetops, she plummets toward the river that swallows her up, then spits her out, spinning her around like a fallen leaf.

Overhead an osprey on majestic black and white wings swoops down to pluck from the river what it detects as a fish feeding near the surface. Largely a fish eater, the river-hawk is accustomed to an easy catch of a more passive prey and is surprised when this flailing and gibbering creature sinks its teeth into its talon. Then suddenly flanked by two angry Sprites with clenched fists, the osprey releases its catch, which falls to the ground and lands in a patch of foxglove.

When Indigo opens her eyes, she is looking up into the towering stems. From behind a jagged leaf, the translucent faces of the two Sprites peek between the violet bell-shaped flowers, utterly amazed to see the wingless one.

CHAPTER EIGHT

Squalls of driving rain are sweeping across the Lullwater while at its edge a white-haired Hobb looks out anxiously. The wind flaps the folds of his robe and the cold rain drenches his fur, yet still he stands searching the darkness for any sign of a rower approaching shore. But he can only see the slanting rain that pockmarks the surface of the dark water—until in a flash of lightning, he sees a slender vessel, adrift and overturned.

Wracked with remorse for every unkind word he has ever said to his daughter, the Duke howls in the direction of the unseen moon.

His distant distress can faintly be heard across the Lullwater by another Hobb's large and sensitive ears. Despite the pouring rain, Sage stops and lifts her snout to howl in response, waiting to identify the howler and the source of its pain. But with another crack of lightning, instinct compels her to run, following Thistle toward Lullwater Bridge.

Into the vast and vaulted space beneath its span, the two rush out of the storm. Thistle's frail body shudders violently with the wet cold that has saturated his skin and seeped into his hollow bones. Being a Hobb, Sage has learned the lore of the wilderness that has kept her kind robust and free since the beginning of time. She rubs Thistle's stem-like limbs briskly between her paws, then rummages in a pile of dried twigs and crumbled leaves blown under the bridge. She chooses a twig of birch, peels off the bark and snaps it in two. Between chattering teeth Thistle complains, "This is no time to be playing around with sticks."

"Playing around, as you call it, is how my ancestors figured out how to survive. So watch and learn, Prigg."

His rain-drenched bristles quivering as he sneezes, Thistle draws closer to watch the Hobb at work who first finds a sharp-edged rock to sharpen the tip of the smaller branch. She then scores a groove down the middle of the other. Placing a pebble beneath one end of the longer branch, she angles it upward so that she can sit with her rump on the ground to keep it steady.

"This, my friend, is how a Hobb makes fire from air."

Firmly holding the sharpened stick between her paws, she places its tip in the groove and begins, lightly at first to push back and forth, back and forth, gaining speed until a thread of smoke arises from the friction at the point of contact. As she applies more pressure, keeping the stick moving quickly, more smoke appears and burnt wood dust gathers at the edge of the groove. Sage nods toward a mound of sapless, crushed brown leaves. "Gather up some of those. Then grab a blade of that dried up grass over there and crumble them together like a nest. That's good. Now come here and hold it steady, steady."

Carefully Sage turns over the grooved stick and with a tap displaces the burning ember into the handheld tinder. She gently blows on it until there is a spark and soon a trickle of flame. With a squeal Thistle drops the burning tinder to the ground. "Silly, Prigg," Sage scolds as she falls to her knees, bracing the mound with her paws. She continues to feed it with her breath until a crackling flame is dancing before them.

Thistle is drawn to its heat but then moves away. "According to Law 387 only servants can handle fire. It's far too dangerous."

"Nonsense. They just don't want you to learn how to survive on your own."

"But why wouldn't they?"

"Because then they couldn't keep you locked up in that tree trunk your whole lives." Sage reaches for the birch bark and shreds it with her claws, making wood shavings that she sprinkles on the fire. Instantly they ignite and curl as the flame is fed and a flume of smoke rises.

Outside in the moonlight raindrops splash and splatter off the rocks while Sage and Thistle sit with their backs to the wall, snugly content, enjoying the heat from the fire—safely sheltered beyond the reach of the storm that is now retreating.

"I must say, I'm impressed," says Thistle. "We never learned that back in the New Order."

"Well, Dale is different. We study law, but we also go out into the forest of Prospect and learn the lore of the wild. "

Sniffing the air, Sage follows her nose just beyond their shelter as Thistle watches her approach the gnarly roots of an oak where clumps of fungus grow in the shape of wooly-headed sheep. With her sharpened stick, she cuts before tugging off fistfuls of the pungent mushrooms.

Sage crosses back to Thistle and places the foraged edibles in his arms. "Here hold onto these." She then moves toward a patch of tall, curling chives. Firmly she grips one thick stem and tugs, falling backward as she yanks a bulb from the mud. She then kneels by a puddle to rinse off the grit.

Her brow twitches with pleasure as she sniffs the garlic that she carries back to their campfire. There on a flat stone, she peels and cuts it up before breaking off pieces of the wild mushroom. Spreading out the ingredients on the edge of a dry leaf, she then snaps a twig in two and hands one to Thistle.

"This is how we dine in the wild."

"You eat twigs?"

"Just do what I do." Thistle watches and imitates Sage who skewers the chunks on the stick and roasts them over the open fire until they are a toasty shade of brown.

Now dry and very hungry, Thistle bites down into the spongy, aromatic mushroom kebab and closing his eyes savors the mouthful that he slowly chews. "You do know, it's against the law for Priggs to fraternize with Hobbs, unless of course you're the governor. She can do what she likes."

"Sure, I know the laws of the New Order, but I live by the Laws of the Lullwater that govern the rest of us— Hobbs and Grobbs, as well as Nohms."

"I've never met a Grobb or a Nohm."

"Locked up, how would you? No loss though, the

Grobbs are cantankerous bunch. Ignorant and stubborn, and they never bathe. The Nohms, on the other hand, are a refined and loving lot who spend their days meditating. They are rarely seen, but if you pass a place in the forest where they chant, you can feel their peacefulness."

"Where do they come from?"

"As different as they are, Grobbs and Nohms, and even the Goblins in these woods, are all descendants of the Ancient Order of Gnomes back in England."

"Do they get along here on the Lullwater?"

"We've all managed to coexist. But the Grobbs stir up trouble from time to time." Sage takes Thistle's empty twig and skewers another chunk of fungus before handing it back to him.

"Thank you, sir."

"Call me Sage," she says extending her paw.

Thistle shakes it with his free hand. "Please to meet you. I'm Thistle."

"You realize, Thistle, that this is probably the first meal shared in the wild between Prigg and Hobb for over four hundred years."

"And why, if I may ask, is that so?"

"When we first arrived here by ship after a long and stormy voyage, we had a serious falling out. But back in England by the River Avon, your ancestors and mine were best of friends. And great friends too of all the farming families."

"You mean Them? Not possible—they're killers, Them and their Beasts."

"Time to start rethinking what they taught you back there. True, greed does grip their hearts—the more they have, the more they want. And them thinking they own the earth has always been a dangerous idea for the rest of us. But they're not all bad. And back in Warwickshire we got on very well with the farmers and the tradesmen, especially the wives and children. And with one in particular. Her name was Mary of Arden. And she was a very good storyteller."

"Stories? They're a waste of words. Language was created to record the Law."

"Now, my friend, you've got that all wrong. It was from Mary the storyteller, that your ancestors first learned to read."

"One of Them taught us to read—impossible."

"If you just listen, you might learn there's a lot they didn't teach you back in the New Order." Thistle holds his empty twig toward Sage who takes it and stabs the last of their foraged food onto it.

"Now, to get back to Mary. Her father was a husbandman, fine fellow Robert Arden, and we Hobbs worked with him on his farm in the parish of Wilmcote, plowing the fields with his eight oxen, making beer in the brewery and cheese in the dairy. There was plenty to do back in those times, and we Hobbs, well, we're workers. Sure, there was the odd prank we liked to play, but we lived to work. That was our pleasure, especially when we settled on the farm of a good man like Robert Arden. And it was he who made sure that Mary, his youngest of eight daughters, learned how to read."

"But how do you know all this?"

"While you Priggs bury your heads in law books day in and day out, we Hobbs study lots of other subjects, like history. And as Robert Arden's farm was the last one where we worked before setting sail, he is fondly remembered by us even today. But it was when Mary grew up and married the son of a tenant on her father's land, that's when you Sprites come into the story."

"Really? But how?" Thistle's wings bristle with excitement to learn more of his own ancestors.

"She and her husband moved to Stratford where with her help, he rose to be High Bailiff. Although for Mary, who lost her first two children soon after birth, those years in town were filled with grief. So when she had a son, she doted on the little boy. In warm weather they would stroll along the River Avon and there pick wildflowers. She'd tell him marvelous stories while he in return rewarded her with such bright laughter that he soon drew one of the river spirits to join him. When Will was barely in breeches, she brought along her hornbook and began to teach him how to read. It was then that one Sprite became very possessive, and she pushed away all the others. Her name was Zinnia, and she would sit perched on his shoulder reciting the letters, right along with him."

"And are you quite certain it was the same language we use for our laws?"

"The very same, but for them it was a musical language, alive with rhythm and full of possibilities. As the boy grew up, Zinnia would meet him by the river and being quick with the rhymes, she would recite them in his ear, and he would string them together like pearls. He called her his muse, and she loved him very much.

Inseparable though they were, toward the end of the summer of 1582 Will, now a young man of eighteen, suddenly stopped coming to see her. The moon waxed and waned until finally one evening, Zinnia heard his boots mashing down the tall grasses, and the sound of a lighter step that she could not recognize.

When she flew to meet her beloved mortal, she stopped. For there was Sweet Will, walking with his arm around the waist of a female, who tilting back her head laughed loudly at his words. Zinnia was livid, and it was what happened next that changed Sprite history forever. Will began to recite their poems, the ones that they had created together, to her. That's when Zinnia landed on his shoulder and whispered angrily in his ear—she's hideous, she's old, how could you? And it was his reply that changed the course of Sprite history."

"What did he say?"

"He said, I love her."

"How do you know if no one was there?"

"Peaseblossom and Cobweb were."

"Who are they?"

"Two nosey Sprites who used to spy on all the others, then they'd gossip up and down the Avon—even to us Hobbs."

"I still don't see what any of this has to do with me."

"Everything, just wait. Zinnia was so furious that she made herself invisible, never to be seen again by Will or any human—though she did continue to watch jealously when the couple strolled along the river. Then in the spring after a child was born, the newly-weds brought her to the riverbank to weave her necklaces and crowns of wildflowers. Being proud, Zinnia kept boasting to the other Sprites that Will would grow tired of the cow as she called her, and that she would be his muse again. But when the cow gave birth to two more calves—a boy and girl, Zinnia despaired. She gave up all hope of ever renewing their bond, and embittered she vowed to never trust one of them again. So instead of poetry, she began writing laws, laws to create a new colony without rhymes or laughter."

"That's the very first law of the New Order of the World: Priggs shall utter no words of poetry or joy."

"And it was Zinnia who wrote it, along with 1,998 others, out of spite and jealousy—there was rumored to be a last law that was never found, but the rest you Priggs still live by."

"Yes, I learned them all by heart."

"Well, it was in these heartless laws that the King saw a way to control the unruly Sprites. And so he married Zinnia and arranged for their passage in the hold of a ship soon to set sail across the Atlantic. It was according to his decree that all the Sprites, who since the beginning of time had frolicked on the River Avon, were eed from Stratford and forced to march to London to board the ship."

"March? Why would they march if back then we had wings?"

"By the King's decree before leaving the old elm, all Sprites were forced to make one last wish, which was to wish away their wings. And of course, their power to wish relied on their ability to fly, and so when they lost their wings, they lost their identity as Sprites. And that's how they came to be Priggs."

"Then how do I still have wings?"

"Well, that's a bit of a mystery, isn't it?"

"How long was this voyage?"

"Three moons appeared and vanished before land was sighted. And though the ship sailed on, the Priggs were forced to disembark. It was a rich and abundant land that they explored until they set down roots in this forest."

"That still doesn't explain how you Hobbs came to live here by the Lullwater."

"Well, being loyal by nature and knowing that wingless you would not last long on sea or land, we

Hobbs boarded the ship to be your guides and protectors. And as useful as we were on Robert Arden's farm in Wilmcote, we proved to be very resourceful in the wild."

"Yes, I can see that," replies Thistle, who now warm and dry with a full stomach, yawns and stretches his wings that sleepily tuck themselves in under his shoulders.

"But after they set up their colony, the Priggs' power went to their heads. First, they forced insects to be servants, and soon after all creatures in the tree trunk were ordered to serve them, too. They then tried to imprison us Hobbs, so we escaped into this ancient forest that surrounds us still. And that is why until tonight Priggs and Hobbs have remained on their own sides of the Lullwater."

A gentle snoring rises from the red oak leaf where curled up by the fire, Thistle has fallen asleep. Poking at the embers to keep them burning, Sage stays awake through the night to protect the sleeping Sprite while on the other side of the Nethermead in the Upper Office, Chief Justice Bitterroot pulls back the leafy drapes to look out at the moon dappled meadow.

CHAPTER NINE

Alone Bitterroot taps the wart on his brow and lifts the scaly lid of his pineal eye, the third eye that he keeps closed in the presence of the Priggs. He is indeed a coldblooded creature, better suited to the swamp than the Upper Office, but only by taking over the New Order can he satisfy his lust for power.

Only now can he prove that his ancestors—disdained, reviled as lowly slimy creepers of the earth—are not only as good as their Old Elm lineage, but by standing upright and walking among them, ultimately subjugating all Priggs to his will, he will prove reptilian superiority. And tonight, here in the empty office, his office, Bitterroot feels a wave of pride swell within him.

Throughout his career he has been forced to pretend to be subservient to the governor when in fact he has known himself to be superior, more learned, more devoted to the letter of the law than any member of the first family. They with their excesses—the governor's indulgence in lavender, the first husband's obsession with golf, long ago outlawed with all other forms of fun and frivolity. And most galling Indigo's disregard for the laws of the New Order.

"Hypocrites," he mutters, but very much pleased at his stealth in undermining the governor's administration in only one day—their precious spoiled offspring with her antics finally ended. And the renegade Martine, destroyed. And then of course he quivers with the added thrill of uncovering the first family's secret—the birth and cover-up of a winged son. How effective this piece of hideous evidence has proven to be in rousing all the Priggs to a fever pitch of hatred—a hatred he can now ignite to utterly destroy the governor upon her return.

"But how can I be sure to blot out any stain of loyalty that they might still have for the first family? After all, they were much loved—and love is a fickle thing that can defy and undermine control."

The chief justice knows that lies like seeds take time to root and sprout and spread. He knows he needs time to be sure he has deeply planted his poison in the mind of every Prigg and that all have been tainted by it. At that moment Bizby flies in through the knothole and waggles a hasty message.

"What? Returning? Tonight, but how can this be so? They are to attend the graduation at Dale."

Bizby continues to waggle the message which Bitterroot quickly decodes but cannot comprehend. He deciphers the exact point where Eon, the ancient snapping turtle assigned to keep watch, reported a disabled boat adrift. The bee also waggles the location of the point on the bank of the Lullwater where the Duke was last sighted, howling with grief. For a moment Bitterroot is stumped. "But what has any of this to do with the governor and the first husband?"

Next Bizby waggles the location where he last sighted their swallows crossing the Lullwater on their return flight from New Hobb.

"But why? Has there been a falling out? Or perhaps the graduation has been cancelled. In any case, this is too soon, far too soon."

Bitterroot is agitated by this news and breathes heavily. He closes the lid of his third eye and wonders how before their arrival at dawn, he can be sure to turn all Priggs against the governor and guarantee his own rise to power without resistance.

"Ah, I have it," Bitterroot muses. "I will send out a message to each and every Prigg. No doubt they will be both honored and terrified to get the alert directly from the Upper Office."

Nearby Bizby hovers and awaits his orders. "Transmit this message to each Prigg. Inform them one by one that I, former Chief Justice now Chief Executive, is placing the elm on Alert Level 5. The winged traitor has escaped to New Hobb where its mother, the governor, is preparing to attack. All must stand ready to fight."

As Bizby flies off, Bitterroot calls after him. "Tell them to be afraid. Be very afraid. The New Order of the World is in grave danger." He then scurries toward the Root System, his thin lips twisting upward in a cruel smile. "And I shall have the pleasure of delivering the message myself to the prisoner."

Bitterroot has a hesitant form of locomotion—close to the curving wall he skitters, stopping to look behind, before hurrying a short distance to stop again. He makes his way down the same passageways where earlier Indigo had been dragged, flicking out his tongue to pick up the smell from the bloodied footprints and the lingering scent of fear.

"Ah, delicious," he says touching the roof of his mouth with the tips of his forked tongue.

When he reaches the open Hatch, he kneels, expecting to hear sobs. Met with silence, he assumes that the tormented Prigg has lapsed into the oblivion of sleep. He smiles at the thought of rousing her to face her powerless and pitiful condition.

"Oh, Indigo. Offspring of the not so blue-blooded as you thought first family." When no whimper rises, he grabs a stone and hurls it down the Hatch. Bitterroot listens as it hits bottom, and a thud echoes upward. Still no sound of the prisoner stirring rises from the crypt.

Designed to ensure that there is no way out of the Root System, neither is there a way in, except to be shoved. Yet his appetite for cruelty has been whetted, and the chief executive desires to see Indigo desperate and groveling for his mercy, which of course he will promise but not give to further enhance the flavor of the pain inflicted.

"A rope, I must find a rope and be lowered into the abyss to see her debased, devalued and utterly dejected." Bitterroot hurries to the upper chambers to summon the SF2, unaware that the prisoner has fallen onto the shore of a distant misty river, far beyond the reach of his treachery where motionless Indigo lies in that other world, flanked by the two chittering Sprites.

CHAPTER TEN

Before dawn the Lullwater is still, disturbed only by
the splash of a largemouth bass feeding on black flies.
Sage steps outside. Her nostrils quiver as she inhales the
cold air, redolent with a blend of water lilies, green grass
and the moist decay of fallen limbs and tree trunks
turning into mulch. She crosses to the pond where she

kneels—sipping, rinsing, loudly gargling before splashing cold water on her face then vigorously shaking off the droplets from her fur.

Her brow furrows and her ears twitch. Sniffing the air, she detects danger that is confirmed by the faint whiff of unwashed Grobbs. Knowing their habit of roiling up trouble around the Lullwater, she returns to rouse Thistle so that they can move on before its arrival. Approaching the campfire, she stops abruptly when she sees the monstrous shadow of a long-legged insect cast against the curving wall and ceiling. As her eyes adjust, she sees that it is looming over her sleeping companion. Grabbing a twig, she ignites its tip in the fire.

"Back off or be cooked to a crisp."

Standing its ground, the green predator raises its raptorial forelegs and hisses with a fury that awakens Thistle who opens his eyes and sees the mantis towering above him. "You're alive," he cries as his wings carry him upward.

Bewildered Sage keeps a firm grip on her torch as Thistle hugs the killer bug. "Are you insane? It'll chomp off your head and devour you whole!"

"Oh, Martine, when Bitterroot said you were dead, I knew he was lying. But where's Indigo?"

As the mantis mimes the scene of the prisoner being dragged in chains by the SF2 with Bitterroot skulking behind them down the dark passageway that leads to the Root System, Thistle's amber eyes burn bright with anger.

"He will pay," he utters—his words obliterated by the growling and cursing of the Grobbs that slithers out of a hole in the hill and along the muddy bank to peer under the bridge.

Known to move through earth like humans move through air or fish water, the Grobbs' hide is caked with various shades of dirt. From its treks—sliding, slithering, tunneling, trotting through the park—bits of twigs and cellophane, tiny turds as well as several bottle caps are embedded between its scales. It has three slack-jawed heads with one bloodshot eye at the center of each—two balanced on its shoulders, one protruding from its chest. Each head has one cavity that is both mouth and nostril, and that is the source of its stench. Known to devour any living or dead thing in its path, its teeth and tongues are layered with years of detritus—bits of sinew, feathers, fur and tortoise shell.

When the serpent raises itself and stands upright, firmly balanced on its wide and muscular tail, its gargantuan form like a gnarled and twisted tree with four limbs blocks the moonlight from the Hobb who steps forward dwarfed but unafraid. "Halt, what business have you here?"

The Grobbs' scaly fingertips snuff out the flame of Sage's torch and raise her, still clinging to the twig, high above the ground. Then all three faces lean forward, leering, enveloping Sage with its foul breath to ask in unison. "What business have we under our own bridge?"

"Now that's a laugh," sneers the face on the left.

"What cheek," snickers the face that glances up from the Grobbs' armored chest, straining its scrawny neck to get a better view of the dangling intruder.

Wildly Sage kicks the air. "Put me down."

"How about right here?" While one gnarly hand drops Sage onto a ridged and rocky palm, another grabs the winged creature flying above the fire. The serpent's third and fourth hands seize them both, closing its fingers around them like the bars of a cage.

Thistle's head emerges from under a thumb. "Let me go, I must return to the New Order. It's a matter of life or death."

"Should've thought of that before illegally entering under our bridge."

Swaying his head then curling his abdomen, Martine leaps onto a boulder. There he raises his spiked forelegs to signal his readiness to fight.

"The mantis is right," whispers Sage. "We must fight."

"No," replies Thistle, underestimating the acute hearing of the Grobbs. "We must rely on patience and guile."

"Patience and Guile? Which one's he?" growls the Grobbs, lunging toward Martine and sweeping the air with its monstrous hand before striking down on the rock with a powerful swat. Thistle and Sage gasp with horror at the swiftness of Martine's destruction.

"You mean, which one was he?" snickers the other.

The third head whines with anticipation. "Let me eat it, oh, do let me eat it. You know how I love mashed mantis."

"I mashed it, it's mine."

All three heads groan when the Grobbs removes its hand from the wall to see that it has missed its mark and that the mantis has escaped.

"Let us go," shouts Sage from between the Grobbs' clenched fingers. "According to the Laws of the Lullwater, I demand our rights!"

Raising its filth encrusted eyebrow, the head nearest Sage stretches away from the chest, tilting its chin toward the brazen stranger and speaks in a high-pitched voice. "Can you believe the cheekiness of this rat?"

"I'm not a rat, I'm a Hobb."

"And how about the yellow one? What's she, a pansy?"

"I'm not a flower. I'm a Prigg."

The head on the left shoulder turns toward the one to its right. "What's a Prigg?"

"Don't matter what it is, it don't belong here!"

"Just asking is all."

"Yeah well, asking is thinking and that's my job!"

"Sirs," Sage calls out, but her voice only reaches the head on the chest while the other two snarl and bicker.

"I am not a sir!"

"Excuse me, madam."

"That's miss!"

"Pardon me, miss, but would you inform the others that we meant no harm. We only stopped here to escape last night's storm."

"Meant no harm?" Turning her head upward, she asks with disgust. "Do you hear that? Come home to find strangers toasting their toes by a fire, and it tells us that it meant no harm."

"Loud and clear. Let me set you straight, rat, this is our territory, Grobbs' territory, no immigrants allowed."

"Without exception," confirms the other.

"Under penalty of law."

Sage wedges her face between the Grobbs' fingers to shout. "According to the inter-colony Law of the Lullwater, we have committed no crime."

"I see it fancies itself a bit of a lawyer," snickers the head jutting out from the ribs.

"Just a bit," says the other.

The head on the right peers down from its rheumy eye. "Just a wee little bit, about the size of my toe with about as much brains as a booger."

"I've enough brains to know that all creatures of this forest have the right to cross the Nethermead."

"Well, you're not on the Nethermead, are you? Not until you cross our bridge—under which I charge you with illegal trespass and sentence you to immediate deportation."

"Yes, let's deport it," cries the other. "Let's tie a stone around its waists and deport it to the bottom of the pond!"

"Too much work. I order them deported down your gullet!"

"That one's too hairy. And the other with those pointy spikes? I'm not putting that thing in my mouth."

"You'll eat it, and that's an order."

"Yeah? And who'll poop it out?"

"All three," complains the head, glancing up from the chest.

"No pain, no gain," growls the head on the right.

As the two heads atop the Grobbs' shoulders continue to quarrel over the fate of the trespassers, Thistle addresses the face closest to him. "Pardon me, miss. But may I ask you a question?"

"Don't go asking for any last wishes—we used to give them, but it's too pitiful, and pity gives me gas."

"No, my esteemed lady," says Thistle in a way that makes its lips soften and bend upward in an unaccustomed smile. "But may I ask you question of a personal nature?"

"I'm not saying I'll answer it, but go ahead, ask."

"Do you have digestive issues?"

"You mean trouble with the pipes?"

"Yes, trouble with the pipes."

"What with the rocks and bark and bones of any

rotted thing these two barbarians devour, who wouldn't?"

"If am to be deported, either way, out of a sense decency I feel obliged to share with you the secret of a little-known homeopathic cure."

"A homeo-what?"

"A medicine."

"Like pills? Came across a bottle of those—nasty little capsules. Almost killed us. Nope. No more pills for me."

"Well, this isn't a pharmaceutical, I mean pill. It's a natural substance that will, over time, heal your digestive system. And it's quite tasty really."

"Tasty?"

"Nutty, smooth—and with an added zest that only the first family has ever been privileged to enjoy."

The head on the left looks downward, its attention drawn in by the word tasty. "And why are you telling us?"

"As you know, these Priggs fancy themselves better than all the creatures of the Lullwater, especially, pardon me for saying so—the Grobbs."

"Is that so?"

"As a former Prigg, I can tell you. I was often offended myself at the way other creatures, particularly you Grobbs, were unfairly ridiculed and maligned."

"Mal-what?"

"They said you were, well, dirty and undeserving of

the better things in life—like this natural substance."

"Savory or sweet?"

"Or is it a mix of the two. I do like salty sweet," says the other, salivating.

"Ah, but being a lowly servant of the first family, I was never allowed to taste it myself—but every time they ate it, I could hear the first family's moans of ecstasy. And they never had, as you say, problems with their pipes."

"Tell us its name," they demand.

Sage looks to Thistle with her eyebrows writhing in confusion, having no idea what her companion has up his sleeve.

"Bitterroot," says Thistle.

"Yes, bitterroot," nods Sage, wholly perplexed.

"Bitterroot? Don't sound so tasty to me."

"Ah, they call it bitterroot so no other creature will crave it. To throw them off, or else they'd be trampling at the roots to get at it."

"I see. Then we Grobbs'll be the first."

"Well, it's quite a long way across the Nethermead. And I know that you're set on deporting us immediately—one way or the other. So, I don't suppose I have time to take you to it."

"Shut it, rat. As detainee, we tell you what to do, not the other way around. And we order you to lead us to the bitterroot."

"If you insist, but please sirs, and my lady. If I may be so bold, given your, shall we say aroma, the Priggs will smell you coming before we are halfway across the Nethermead—and the first thing they will do is lock up the bitterroot."

"We smell?"

"Distinctly," responds Sage, catching on to the game.

The Grobbs look equally confused and perhaps for the first time in its existence ashamed.

"Well, how does one reduce one's smell. We are after all the Grobbs, and we smell like the Grobbs."

"You don't have to, you know. It's called bathing. It's quite pleasant. You just sort of inch out into the Lullwater and paddle around a bit, rub at your cheeks, all eight of them. Then lap up a little water to swish around your teeth, and when you emerge, you will have most definitely reduced the smell of Grobbs."

Keeping the fingers of two hands encaging the prisoners, the Grobbs takes hold of a branch of an overhanging willow. Gingerly it inches out into the dark pond, squealing with delight at its first touch of water. Grinning with satisfaction, Thistle winks at Sage who shrugs.

"Okay, so? Now we'll be devoured later rather than sooner by a slightly less filthy Grobbs."

"Now it will slither and trot across the Nethermead faster than we could have gotten there by wing or foot!"

"If I'm not mistaken, last night you clearly were headed in the opposite direction. Why do you want to go back there now?"

"To save Indigo."

"Who's Indigo?"

"My twin who has been wrongfully imprisoned."

"Then, by all means we must," replies Sage whose courageous nature has long been smothered by the uneventful life she has led as a law student of Dale. "I will be honored to accompany you on your quest. But what happens when we get there and there is no bitterroot?"

"But there is." Thistle smiles. "Bitterroot beyond belief!"

CHAPTER ELEVEN

Old Order of the World 1587

In the tall grass on the bank of the River Avon, Peaseblossom and Cobweb giggle and gossip, pointing their dazzling fingers and snickering at the fallen creature's garments—a robe and breeches like the mortals wear, looking as silly on the bluish creature as if a cat had appeared in boots and a wide-brimmed hat.

They themselves wear no clothes, for like birds or flowers they have no need—no vulnerability to temperature, no need to ward off wind or rain, being made of the same natural components as dewdrops, snowflakes, or light itself—shimmering by day, disappearing in darkness, dimly but proportionately aglow with the waxing and waning moon.

They also cannot sicken or die, and so they are baffled by the wingless one whose face and size resemble their own, but who lies in the grass like an injured fledgling fallen from a nest. Curious one swoops from where they hide behind the blossoms of fox glove to hover above it.

"Nay, Cobweb! Do not go so near. 'Tis surely cursed, a thing to fear."

"Oh, Sprite, thou doth fear everything. How can it catch me if it hath no wings?"

Taking a twig from the ground, Cobweb pokes the creature that groans and draws its legs to its chest and rolls onto its side. When in the breeze that jostles the buds and blossoms, the leaves of its tunic flutter away, both Sprites gasp. Stunned they stare at its bare back where two bumps swell and pulse with life beneath its skin.

"This thing is weird. Let's fly away and leave it on the ground."

"But surely 'twill be eaten by a hungry fox or hound."

Taking pity on the wingless one, Peaseblossom

gathers a mound of grass and petals to conceal it from any passing predator. Then when one eye of the fallen creature flutters open, she recognizes that they are the same.

"Come, let us fly to Zinnia our Queen, and to her unfold this strange thing we have seen."

Side by side the river spirits fly toward the old elm on the edge of Arden farm. But when from the church tower in Stratford, the bell rings out the hour, Cobweb changes course to veer instead toward town. Chasing him, Peaseblossom grabs hold of his wing.

"Whoa, Cobweb, whither doth thou stray?"

"Let's tarry first to High Street for today is market day."

"To flit away our time when we have news to bear?"

"Oh, cousin, come! A merrier hour was never wasted there."

Leaving the wingless one hidden beneath the grassy mound, Cobweb and Peaseblossom detour toward the market town where they flit through the streets of Stratford-upon-Avon. With great anticipation they turn onto High Street where shopkeepers and vendors from the countryside sell their wares—soap, candles, butter, oil, herbs and fruits both fresh and dried, as well as clucking hens, grunting pigs and Dragon's Milk, a heady home-brewed ale.

There a third and impish Sprite zigzags among the townspeople where he pinches earlobes, flicks noses and lands on the wide brim of a milkmaid's straw hat to clutch his sides and sputter with laughter.

"Ho over hither, Robin Goodfellow," calls Cobweb to the much-admired Sprite also known as Puck, who darts downward to land on the stone base of the High Cross, a structure built to designate this busy marketplace.

"How now, brother, what mischief doth thee make?"

With a wink Cobweb darts beneath the timbers of a stall where a farmer's wife sells apples, turnips and potatoes. When he nudges an apple from the cart, an avalanche of fruit and vegetables follows, thudding and bouncing off the cobblestones. In a flash the irate merchant reaches out her thick-fingered hand, grabs the collar of a passing boy and with the other pummels his head and shoulders as he tries to fend off her heavy blows.

"Stop her," cries the kind-hearted Peaseblossom.

Swooping in between the attacker and her innocent victim, Puck grabs the hem of the woman's dirty apron and pulls it up and over her eyes. He then nips the fat hand that releases the boy who runs down an alley.

"Well done, Robin," calls Peaseblossom as her hero flies off over thatch and tile rooftops and heads for Old Elm. She turns to follow him when she sees a familiar townsman with a small boy on his shoulders. She waves to Cobweb who flies after her to catch up with the mortal. Flanking his softly bearded cheeks, together they greet him. "Hail, mortal!"

"How now, spirits! Whither wander you?"

Somersaulting before his dark eyes, Cobweb chants. "Over hill, over dale, through bush, through brier. Over park, over pale, through flood, through fire."

"We do wander everywhere, swifter than the moon's sphere to Zinnia our fairy queen."

"As always well sung, my muses. And how fares your Queen?"

"Since her marriage to the King, not well at all," says Peaseblossom blushing. "We all wish that she had married you, Will."

"Ah, Zinnia and I are wed in words. A marriage that will outlive us both. Will you tell her that for me?"

"Then give us some token so that she will know that we are not lying."

"Send her this." Will kisses his fingertip and places it gently on Peaseblossom's cheek as his little son, giggling, does the same to Cobweb who rubs it off as if it were a smudge of dirt. Delighted the boy laughs more loudly, placing a second kiss on his finger, which to Cobweb's indignation he pokes beneath his wings so that the kiss is out of reach. "Fare thee well, gentle Sprites. Hamnet's mother will be much offended if we are late for midday meal!"

With the boy bouncing on his shoulders and hanging onto two tassels of his hair like reins, Will trots down Henley Street while the river spirits follow, one at each *ear.*

Rapidly Peaseblossom flaps her wings to keep up with his long-legged stride. "Oh, sweetest poet Will, as Zinnia once called thee, hie thee hence to her who dotes on you devotedly."

"Since last she called me that fair name, the Queen has called me worse. Now wantonly she outlaws joy and makes a crime of verse!"

"Forgive her, Will, and make amends so that thy heartless feud might end."

"Inform the Queen it is my lot as mortal to lead a mortal's life."

At the door of a sprawling house, constructed of oak beams and plaster, appears a woman whose sharp eyes narrow first on Will and then on the Sprites. Raising a wooden spoon still steaming with the gravy of a stew recently stirred, she addresses them sternly. "Recall the clout you got, when from my milk you stole the cream? So, get thee gone now, impish sprites, lest from thine eyes thy tears will stream."

"Why stay you, Will, with a shrewish wife when with our Queen you'd have a wondrous life?"

Taking his son from his shoulders, he places Hamnet in his mother's arms before turning toward the Sprites and bowing with a flourish. "Soon from this town I shall turn away my eyes. To seek new friends and stranger companies. Farewell, sweet playfellows."

"Peaseblossom, let's take leave of this poetic knave,

and of his lost affection, no memory be saved!" Fleeing their once beloved mortal and the grumbling of his angry wife, the Sprites resume their rambling flight toward the old elm where, since her abandonment of Will, Queen Zinnia has worked in her chamber day and night.

Once the most carefree and fun-loving of the Sprites, she has with her unhappy marriage to the King begun to wither. With her decreasing luminosity, her colors have faded, and her wings have weakened as she has no use for them anymore—no dipping, no diving, no flitting, no flying—dancing on dew drops a dim memory of her abandoned youth.

Instead Zinnia spends her days writing with a tiny quill made from the feather of a fledgling swan, dipped in blackberry ink. Barely nourished on sips of rainwater and shreds of dandelion leaves, her body has begun to feed on itself and her birdlike bones protrude under her sallow skin. She works barely glancing up from the scroll before her, concocting restrictive laws for the colony to be called the New Order of the World that her husband has decreed will be established in a new land.

When the King enters, she does not look up from her parchment. Too late she has realized her mistake. That by marrying the King, bedazzled by his power that she thought she would share, she has only given up her own independence and become no more than a drone. And even the laws which in her anger and jealousy she was at first impassioned to write, now have no hold on her imagination, just as the King has no hold on her heart.

With the sound of his massive wings folding, the King flies through the hole in the sapwood to land with a jarring thud on the floor. With long strides he crosses the room to stand with his white-gloved hands on his hips, looming over Zinnia as she writes. When he brings down his fist on her desk, she flinches as one accustomed to the threat of kicks and blows.

"It is settled. We will set sail from London, make ready to leave at dawn." As luminous as are the other Sprites, indeed as Zinnia used to be, the King absorbs the same rays which in him converge to form a dense shadow, ominous as the mouth of a cave on a bleak and moonless night. "Have you written the last law?"

Zinnia casts down her eyes. "Not yet, my lord."

"Then finish. All are assembled to wish away their wings."

"What if they refuse, my lord?"

"Refuse? You yourself drafted the prohibition to refusal. And I have already signed it into law."

"Yes, my Lord, but how will we convince them to accept these laws. You know how free-willed these Sprites are by nature, how intent they are to follow their own whims."

"Yes, their whims and nature must be crushed. First by fear. They have been forewarned that aboard the ship

113

winged creatures are prone to deadly disease, and therefore, to ensure their safe passage, they must wish them away."

"But, my Lord, as you agreed, we will retain ours, so that we can wish them back when the need arises."

"As Priggs they will have no need of wings." The King departs the chamber to do the deed that will deprive all generations of their wings, rending them powerless against him and his descendants' control. With a wave of nausea, Queen Zinnia is overwhelmed with remorse for the choices she has made—choices that now are marching like disillusioned soldiers toward a doomed battlefield. Like a well-aimed spear, her memory pierces her conscience, and she recalls her cruel and unkind words to Will and her unwillingness to accept that his human life like hers had to take its natural course.

With a flash of intuition, she picks up her quill and dips it into the small pot of blue-black ink. Atop the parchment she writes, the Last Law of the New Order of the World as decreed by Queen Zinnia. Quickly she composes the lines on which she makes a powerful wish. Flapping her wings defiantly, she wishes the words to life, a life that will transcend her own and keep the Spites of a future generation inspirited and free. Reaching for a pinch of dust from a hollow seed, she sprinkles it on the scroll to dry the ink. "Although this is the last law I shall pen, in future generations it will make them free again."

Gently she shakes the parchment then rolls up the scroll that will preserve one law to supersede all others. Around it she ties a blade of grass and is about to begin packing for the inevitable voyage when down the corridor she hears a terrible keening. The wailing of the Sprites rises in a dark swell that floods the old elm with their sorrow and their grief—for she knows the King has deceived them into wishing away their wings.

By her desk stands the empty, open trunk. Leaning over it, she feels the nectar within her rise, and as she heaves into its leather lining, she weeps a river of remorse. Mesmerized she watches her own tears flow into a figure eight—gushing to the east, then to the west, then circling eastward again. When she hears the King's heavy footfalls, she wipes away her tears as he enters. Clapping his gloved hands with a dull thud, he smiles broadly. "The deed is done. Now wish away your wings, and we will depart."

"But, my Lord, you promised. We were to retain our wings—so together we would rule and protect the wingless Priggs."

"Only my wings will be needed now. I command you to wish away your own."

"But I can't, I won't," she stammers, rising from her seat.

"Then if you will not wish them away, I will take them by force."

The emaciated wings quiver with fright as the King

reaches behind the Queen who struggles to escape his grasp. He shoves her to the ground, then grabs and squeezes them with such force that he crushes their web work of fragile bones before muttering a hateful curse to obliterate them.

Forever.

Wrenching them from her back, he throws them to the ground where they pulse with their faint and final breaths of life. Zinnia gasps and swallows the pain that wracks her body and the agony that assaults her soul while with bitter laughter, the King leaps from the knothole and flies into the night.

Huddled on the floor with her knees pulled toward her palpitating chest, the Queen is no longer translucent, but instead made of solid flesh with her many colors faded to a dull and bluish grey. When she hears the flutter of approaching wings, ashamed of her wingless body, she hides beneath a jagged oval leaf. Above her hover the two disobedient Sprites, who instead of attending the King's assembly were dallying along the river.

"My Queen," says Peaseblossom. "A creature has fallen from the sky—it seems to be dying."

"Yes, what of it? That is the way of all corporeal beings. And that is all we are now." In the darkness the Sprites cannot see the Queen's discarded wings upon the ground. But feeling theirs fan the air, Zinnia looks up through swollen eyes to see their bright figures above her. *"Peaseblossom? Cobweb? Were you not at the assembly? His Majesty will be furious."*

"What majesty? We know no majesty," says Cobweb folding his arms defiantly.

"Unless you mean the majesty of the sky or the river or the air in between."

"Yes, that majesty we know, and we were out honoring Her majesty when we came upon a most unnatural sight."

"My lady, it is like us, yet different—'tis a wingless one."

"I say to leave it like a weak, rejected bird to die."

"I say let it live," pleads Peaseblossom.

"We are all beyond help now," murmurs the Queen who shifts under the leaf to face the wall. But when the blended melody of blackbirds, robins, wrens and warblers rises over Wilmcote, she knows that with the dawn the King will come to lead them to London where they will be forced to board the ship. Knowing what her two beloved friends will suffer, she snaps out of her despair. As she dashes to her desk, the leaf that concealed her wounds falls to the floor. Peaseblossom gasps to see that her back is bare and bruised, and where once had been two lavish wings, there are two purple gashes.

"My Queen, what has he done to you?"

"Only that which I myself allowed when I turned my back on poetry and penned the laws that made it a

crime."

"Tis not too late," says Cobweb, "we will fight."

"Tis not too late, says Peaseblossom, "we will sing."

"No time," she says pressing the scroll into Peaseblossom's hands. "Be well, my darlings, and when the time is right, read this the last law and tell our descendants that it must be their first. Tell them that Queen Zinnia commands them to live free without fear." On the branch outside her chamber, the voice of the King rings out orders to the woeful, wingless Sprites who have assembled outside the tree to begin the long march to London.

"Quickly, hide in here." She shoos the sprites into the trunk who obediently swoop downward, their size diminishing and their voices growing faint as they descend.

"We go, we go; look how we go, swifter than arrow from the Tartar's bow!"

Zinnia shuts the domed lid of the trunk and turns the key in the padlock, knowing that with their own wings Peaseblossom and Cobweb will wish themselves a better world by the banks of the river of her tears. Quickly she crosses to the knothole where she tosses away the key.

CHAPTER TWELVE

Flanked by the SF2, Bitterroot scutters back down the labyrinthine channels first bored into the sapwood by elm-bark beetles and later widened for the passage of Priggs and the creatures who serve them. Bitterroot leads the agents that drag a length of ivy from which the leaves have been plucked. Standing by the Hatch,

Bitterroot reaches for one end that he binds around his reptilian body and weaves it into a tight knot.

"Lower me down slowly. When I tug twice, pull me back up." The assassin bugs obey. As the temperature drops with his descent, the spongy tissue confined within the thin wall of his heart beats more slowly. Accustomed to darkness, Bitterroot feels no fear as deeper into the abyss he descends—salivating with the excitement of soon witnessing his prisoner's pain.

"Indigo," he calls. "I do hope you find your new lodgings suitable for a member of the former first family." He laughs with maniacal pleasure that echoes through the dank cell as his claws touch the ground. "Indigo?"

When there is no response, he fears that he may be too late. Could she have already died, broken and abandoned? Might he have been cheated of the chance to see Indigo grovel for his mercy? Enraged at the possibility of the premature death, he kicks about in the darkness to locate the cadaver, only to trip over the edge of another portal. For a moment leaning left to regain his balance, he cries out at the sight of the sputtering light diving toward his head before he stumbles into the hole, falling beyond the length of ivy that binds him to his agent. The vine snaps, and with a jolt Bitterroot hits bottom.

He flails his short arms in the whorls of silvery blue mist and screams. "Help, help, get me out of here!"

Standing far above, the SF2 can faintly hear his cries, but when the agent who holds the slack stem hauls it upward to find the knotted end untethered from the chief justice, he lets go. With a quick communication between them, the assassin beetles skitter back up the twisted tunnels and out the first knothole into the night.

Cursing, Bitterroot stumbles into a heavy object. From it stream waves of shimmering clouds. Through the gauzy light, he sees a pile of bones from which arise two skeletal hands. He draws back as toward him they float with outstretched fingers that wrap around his neck. Throwing himself downward, he grapples with the bones, prying them off his scaly skin until they clatter to the ground. Then where his tail had been, he feels a pulsing sensation. He scans the floor in dread where, indeed, he sees it twitching beside him, oozing blood.

"Help! Help me!" he cries into the void. Only Bizby, who senses his distress, makes a beeline from the upper chambers, down the Hatch and into the Root System. "Ah, my loyal messenger. I feared I had been abandoned. What news have you?"

Bizby waggles the exact location of the governor and her husband whom he has sighted landing on the sill of their chamber.

"So, the traitors have returned. Inform the Priggs we are at war. Order all citizens to seek and destroy the enemy within." While Bizby flies off to carry out his orders, Bitterroot squats beside his severed tail, stroking it gently and whispering. "Let us wait and watch the drama unfold. War—the word alone will stun the Priggs into total submission." At his touch the tail inches closer and climbs into his arms. "Yes, soon Bizby will return with news of the governor's final destruction—and all will be mine. My Upper Office, my Priggs, my New Order of the World."

As each Prigg is informed of war and the current danger of the enemy's presence, each face grows pale with fear. Hypnotized by that one word, they leave their niches and file down the corridors to stand silently outside the governor's door, awaiting the moment it will open. Inside Winston is standing on the sill removing his golf bag from the swallow's beak. Beside him the governor surveys the chamber, her feathered gown rumpled and her face travel-worn, wringing her hands fretfully. "I'm telling you, Winston, something's not right."

"Nonsense, dear, we've come home early, unannounced. No one is even up yet."

"Winston. I sense we are in danger."

"That's just your intuition getting the best of you. All's well in the elm. Now have some lavender, that will calm you down."

"No, I will not calm down. I am going to check on Indigo," she says, crossing toward the door.

"And Thistle. Remember our decision. From now on, he is to be included as a full member of this family."

"Yes, Winston. It was heartbreaking to see how the Duke in a few short hours lost his child. We are so fortunate that both of ours are safe in their beds."

"Yes, sad situation for the Duke, tragic really," replies Winston, wiping the morning dew from his golf clubs. "But we're home now. Nothing to fear here in the New Order."

"Well, I'll just go peek in on them."

At the sound of the governor's approaching footsteps, a current of tension runs through the awaiting crowd. All eyes watch the knob turn. When the hinges creak and a crack of light from the chamber falls across the corridor, like a typhoon making landfall, the surge of Priggs overwhelms the governor and floods the Upper Office.

"Desist," cries Winston, swinging his best driver that snaps in two and falls to the floor when he is wrestled to the ground.

The deluge of Priggs carries them out of the room, washing the couple away from their former lives of privilege, a way of life they only now know had been but the tip of a melting icicle. Swept upward by the silent, seething mob, they are driven up the stairwells of the elm. Like a many-fingered beast, the mob rips at the old couple's leafy garments before shoving them onto the uppermost branch into the cold and misty darkness before dawn.

From within the trunk, trembling with anticipation

and terror, they watch the governor and her husband stand on the brink of exile.

Wholly bewildered by this betrayal, the governor can only ask, "But why?" The Priggs, shocked themselves by the velocity of these events, stand ashamed and silent.

Then knowing that the submissive Priggs could never have initiated such action, Winston calls out, "Who put you up to this?"

It is Bizby who responds, waggling the location of Bitterroot who awaits news of their annihilation in the lowest level of the Root System. Winston scowls. Then disrobing before the mob in the same way his son had done the day before, he cries, "Fie on Bitterroot!"

"Winston, no," murmurs the governor.

"What better time than this, my love," he shouts, ripping apart the vine laces that bind his corset, giving full rein to a pair of massive, robust wings.

The slack jawed Priggs fall back, fearful at this display of power. Sweeping up his wife in his arms, Winston leaps into the air. Wide-eyed the Priggs watch the couple soar beyond the canopy—much higher than they have ever flown on the backs of their swallows, higher than the red-tailed hawk that swoops downward to avoid the strange two-headed bird.

"Open your eyes, my dear," says Winston his voice blending with the rush of wind and his pumping wings.

Once the most powerful leader of all the colonies on the Lullwater, without her servants, citizens and an elm to rule, the former governor trembles and squeezes her lids more tightly shut. "Winston, I can't. I'm frightened."

"You simply must, my dear. From this height it's truly unbelievable!" When timidly she opens her eyes, she faces the stars that can be seen through a thin, shifting veil of clouds. Then glancing over her shoulder, she gasps at the grandeur of the view—the vast shadowy acres and cobalt blue waterways.

"There's the Lullwater. And see how it twists and turns and flows into that wide and glorious lake. No wonder Indigo found it irresistible to climb outside the elm to breathe this air and take in all this."

"Winston, we must go back for Indigo. And for Thistle."

"Have no fear, Winnie, we will be together again, only this time not as the first family, but as one family."

Far below Winston sights a monstrous three-headed serpent lumbering toward the elm of the New Order. Sensing danger, he continues to circle overhead, observing its movement without disturbing the governor who lies back in his arms, amazed at the vastness of the sky and her own smallness in the design of Nature.

CHAPTER THIRTEEN

Jostled by the uneven gait of the Grobbs trotting over the Nethermead, Thistle wraps his long, skinny arms around a gnarly thumb while Sage grips the finger beside him. When she sniffs the air, she looks up and points to where a wide-winged bird with two heads circles over the treetops. "I'd worry about that if we weren't with these yahoos."

All three of the Grobbs' eyes narrow and twitch at the apparent insult.

"Who they calling yahoos?"

"Who's calling who what?"

"It's the cheeky one again, calling us yahoos."

"What's a yahoo?"

At the sound of the Grobbs' gnashing teeth, Sage quickly flips her words. "One who-ya feel proud to know. A very clever fellow."

"Or a beautiful maiden," Thistle adds.

"I thank you, kind sir," croons the head whose cheeks, now partially cleansed and visible beneath the dirt, blush faintly.

"Don't fall for the pansy's flattery, you're as ugly as you ever were."

Having been softened by Sage's compliment, the first that a Grobbs has ever heard, the third face now cringes with the sting of the insult, wrinkling up with hurt and self-loathing. A plump tear rolls down its cheek and pools in the folds of the Grobbs' hand.

"You've gone and made her cry," says the head on the left. "Why'd you have to go and do that?"

"Don't want any of us getting all la-di-da about ourselves."

"And why not?" shouts Sage at the lofty, leering head. "Why not let her be a little grand? Maybe you'd stop being such a useless bully!"

The Grobbs snarls in response, its grey-green gums

glistening in the purplish light of predawn that tints the Nethermead. "Who you calling a bully?"

"You!" the others shout back.

"Me? It's the two of you I'm always looking out for. It's always you Grobbs first and me last."

"Looking out for us first? Now that's a laugh."

"It's us you order around day in and day out. It's get up, sit down, bite this, swallow that, never a please."

"Never a thank you. Just shut up and do like you're told."

"Why don't you try voting?" Sage suggests diplomatically.

All three heads turn toward the Hobb. "What's voting?"

"Well, as I've studied, in a true democracy it means each citizen has an equal say. So, when it comes time to make a decision, majority rules. At least that's the way it's supposed to work."

"What's majority?"

"In your case two against one."

"That'll never work," growls the head on the right.

"Why not?"

"I won't win."

"Maybe you shouldn't," says Sage.

"Maybe I should shut you all up!"

The bickering of the Grobbs ends abruptly when the two-headed creature descends toward them and a voice calls out, "Stop, in the name of the New Order of the

World!" Winston's wide wings cast a wavering shadow over Sage and Thistle, held captive in the Grobbs' hand. The rush of air from his wingbeats rustles his son's many-hued bristles that glisten with dew. "Thistle?"

"And Sage, the Duke's daughter," cries the governor craning her head to gaze down in astonishment. "But where is Indigo?"

"Bitterroot has taken her prisoner to the Root System," Thistle shouts to be heard above the whoosh of his father's wings. "We're going to rescue her now."

"And what is this grotesque creature?"

"Yeah, well, I was just about to ask the same of you!" growls the Grobbs, striking out with a powerful clout that Winston dodges, gracefully averting the attack. "Kill, devour!" the head on the right orders.

"Stop! These are members of the first family. And no one knows Bitterroot better!"

"Oh, do please hurry," the governor pleads. "We must save Indigo."

"Ignore those louts, dearie. I understand a woman's heart. I'll help you save your child."

"Oh, thank you, sir."

"Miss," the Grobbs corrects her gently, her face glowing with a new sense of compassion.

"Yes, of course, miss."

Winston flies low alongside the palm where Thistle stands, admiring his father's wings. "So, you have them, too?"

"Like father, like son."

"Then it is true," replies Thistle whose voice betrays the sadness of having been neglected, forced to live in his solitary niche, ashamed of a secret that he now sees his father has shared.

"Oh, Thistle, I am sorry about all this. I should never have agreed to lie to you. I failed you as a father."

"And sadly I, too," says his mother with downcast eye. "We both failed you."

"No such thing as failure, just Nature taking her course. And if she can't get there this way, she'll go another."

Perplexed, the former governor glances toward her husband. "I'm not sure we understand, son."

"Not now, but you will!"

Their search party crosses through a thicket of trees then approaches the elm still shrouded in the darkness of its dense layers of leaves. At the iron fence that surrounds the New Order, the Grobbs stops.

"So, where's this bitterroot?"

Thistle points beyond the Iron Bars toward the serpentine roots. "Down there."

"And how's a Grobbs supposed to get to the bitterroot with this bloody fence in the way?"

"I've heard it told that the Grobbs' most powerful jaws can bite through anything," says Sage. "A very scary prospect to all the inhabitants of the Lullwater."

"Is that so? The Grobbs is feared, is that what you're

telling me?"

"Oh, yes. And chomping through the Iron Bars will show them all just how truly dangerous you are."

"You heard the rat," says the head on the right. "Get to work."

"What about voting, like the rat said?"

"I'll vote you off that shoulder with the back of my hand if you don't shut up!"

"Oh, do please stop bickering," frets the former governor. "You're wasting time, and we must save Indigo!"

"Allow me, Madame," replies the head nearest the heart who leans forward to ferociously bite and gnaw into the iron with sparks and metal splinters flying around them until the space is wide enough for the Grobbs to enter.

A sudden cry of victory reverberates through the twisted branches. The Grobbs glances up at the hundreds of Priggs who are leaning out the knotholes and cracks in the tree, cheering at the destruction of the Iron Bars that they mistakenly have believed held them captive. As they climb outside, many for the first time in their Priggish lives, they scamper onto the leafy limbs and let out a second more joyous cry at the sight of Martine who is flying toward them. Landing on a knobby burl, he raises his raptorial legs to signal his readiness for battle which sets off even more impassioned cries.

"Look, Martine has returned."

"He's alive!" they shout joyously.

Thistle's wings carry him upward to join the mantis that he hugs before climbing onto his back. Propelled by the combined force of their wings, they rise to the uppermost branch where a once fearful tutor, now a courageous Sprite, shakes his fist in the air to raise another shout of solidarity.

So loud and impassioned are the cries that they rock the elm down to its roots, and upon hearing them Bitterroot's small heart flutters while he strokes his truncated tail. "Finally, the war has begun!" Buried deep below the earth, he cannot see that his brief stint of control has ended. However, his look of arrogant self-satisfaction fades at the sound of chomping, slobbering and the splintering of wood. He trembles to hear his own name muttered by an approaching enemy.

"That bitterroot better be in there."

"Do let me have the first bite."

"When it comes to bitterroot, it's every Grobbs for himself."

Fearfully, Bitterroot looks around and, seeing no escape, climbs into the ancient trunk, closing the lid over him.

While the Grobbs chews through the wood, far above Thistle and Martine enter the knothole where the Priggs continue to clamor, making room for their passage as they descend toward the Root System.

Having shaken off the dull stupor of fear and invigorated by their heroes' return, all join in the rescue. Upon reaching the Hatch, they halt and watch silently while Martine and Thistle fly into the abyss.

A thin blue vapor rises from the deepest cell of the Root System, illuminating their path down a sloping passageway. There they are met by two skeletal hands that beckon them to approach the ancient trunk that is slightly ajar. As the bones pry open the lid, more silvery clouds billow from its depths, barely concealing a cowering lizard that clings to its quivering tail.

His jaw throbbing, Martine grabs Bitterroot's head in his raptorial claws, twisting it to a better position for its consumption. Then suddenly, for a reason Thistle cannot yet know, Martine releases his prey. Bitterroot jumps up from his hiding place and runs toward the hole, faintly aglow with the first light of day. From within Thistle shouts to the Grobbs, "There is your Bitterroot!"

"So small?" it asks, kneeling and leering into the hole.

"Follow him, and it will lead you to more."

While the Grobbs chases the slinky reptile toward the Lullwater, Thistle turns toward Martine who stands with the limp and lifeless body of Indigo lying in his raptorial forelegs.

CHAPTER FOURTEEN

All eyes are on the mantis who steps from the Root System bearing the body—lifeless as an abandoned beehive or last year's leaves, a trampled flower or a newborn bird fallen from its nest onto the cold, unyielding ground—a body devoid of being. No word is spoken—neither Indigo's parents, nor her brother can utter a sound. Barely a sigh is exhaled from the Priggs who peer from the limbs of the aged elm. Then like a wind gathering force through the treetops, a gasp turns into a howl that shakes the leaves and bends the grasses, spreading over the Lullwater, drawing forth all the insects and birds, rodents and even the larvae whom Indigo in her lifetime had befriended. The governor clasps Thistle and holds him close, her grief rising from within and washing over him with her tears of regret. Martine places Indigo with her long blue locks dangling toward the ground into the outstretched arms of her father whose weeping can be heard above all the other mourners.

Suddenly from the gouged-out roots, a flash of light shoots above their heads and spins into the form of a silvery dandelion that showers down its seeds. All watch mesmerized by the shimmering cascade of sparks that spin and spiral to form a bird whose beating heart can be seen within the cage of its transparent ribs.

As the phantom bird flies above the Lullwater, a light rain begins to fall. The droplets create a symphony of concentric rings on its surface, pattering on lily pads and the cattails that fringe the pond—and a father whose child stirs in his arms.

All watch as Indigo rises. Awakening as if from sleep, she stretches and sits up, amazed to see her family—all three entwined in an embrace—while the Priggs stream from the elm to gather around them. When Thistle takes hold of Indigo's hands, their combined light illuminates the faces of all the Priggs who look on bewildered.

"Oh, Thistle, I have had a most rare vision. I thought I was..."

"A Sprite?"

"Oh, yes. And I thought I had..." Indigo's eyes widen when Thistle turns his back, and she sees the light that passes through his wings, refracting into brilliant waves of color. "So, it is real. I am, you are, we're Sprites!"

"Yes," says her father holding Indigo's cheeks between his hands and kissing her forehead, his own wings fluttering with the thrill of this family reunion.

"Pop, your wings—they're awesome."

"Well, after being bound up for all those years, when I finally released them, they did plump up rather nicely," Winston replies, glancing over his shoulder. "As Nature intended them to be."

"But why did you hide them for so long?" asks Thistle. "And make me hide mine?"

"I am sorry, son. But over the generations, as Priggs we kept a lot of secrets—although now it does seem time to tell."

"Yes, Winston, do," his wife encourages him. "They need to know."

"Well, back in Old Elm, before the Sprites were forced to board the ship to sail across the Atlantic, the King convinced them to wish away their wings.

However, when Queen Zinnia refused to wish away her own, he forcibly removed them."

Cries rise from the throng of Priggs—bully, brute, tyrant!

"Indeed, he was. Which was why in the New Order of the World when Zinnia gave birth to a son, she swaddled him to hide his tiny wings. And for several years, she managed to keep the secret until one day the King saw the child being bathed and became enraged. Since he could not wish the wings away, he demanded that Zinnia tell the boy to do so. When she refused, he exiled her to the Root System. Over time the King convinced his son that they were useless things, until finally he became ashamed and wished them away himself."

"But the King lied!"

"As rulers often do to get their way. And in the case of this King, his only wish was to have power and rule over an elm of wingless Priggs. But Nature has a way of trumping tyrants, and in future generations wings kept popping up in the family."

"So that's how I was born with mine."

"Yes, Thistle, and I mine. But we are the first to claim them proudly."

All the Priggs listen attentively to the tale—a tale which ignites a spark in each of their hearts, but only one has the courage to step forward to speak. "But what about us? We want our wings back, too."

"As you know," replies Winston, "no one can wish away your wings, but a Sprite can help you get them back."

"Let me, I'll do it," shouts Indigo. Then turning toward the Priggs, she adds, "but you have to believe."

"Believe in what?"

"Believe in who you truly are," she says before blasting upward and circling above their heads, improvising her first wish.

"Believe in blue, below and above—
sky, rain and sea, one river of love.
Believe in the elm, the old and the new—
Look into your heart to find what is true."

So long divided by fear and self-doubt, the Priggs turn to one another to smile and nod, knowing now that they are the same. As Indigo continues to chant, her voice ripples the surface of the Lullwater.

"Believe in Nature whose gifts we adore—
Sing praise to her beauty,
and your wings she'll restore!"

A hush falls over the Nethermead as for one split second, the constant conversations of the forest cease— the chirping of crickets, the chatter of squirrels, the buzz of bees' wings and all the birdsong variations— suspended by Nature to honor this moment of rebirth. Squirming like molting cicadas, the Priggs shed their leafy tunics as their wings begin to sprout.

"Oh, my," says the former governor who feels a mild

throb beneath her shoulder blades as the tips of hers poke through the feathers of her gown.

"Oh, dear, they do suit you," says Winston with admiration while all around them the Priggs are twisting and twirling, trying to catch a glimpse of their own delicate wings.

Like a sudden shower, laughter rains down from the elm where Robin Goodfellow appears. He leaps from the limb and somersaults midair, then points at the Priggs who flap their untrained wings that barely raise them off the ground, driving them left and right as they collide into each other.

"Oh, what fools these fairies be that bump and thump most recklessly!"

"Robin," scolds Indigo. "Don't be a hater. We'll have to teach them sooner or later."

A screech draws all eyes upward where a red-tailed hawk perches. All watch it release the limb from its talons, pushing off on strong legs to soar in wide circles over the Nethermead where a scurry of squirrels scrambles up tree trunks and hundreds of starlings rise from the branches. Creating a cloud of rhythm, together the birds drive off the predator as they fly in perfect coordination. Some lean left while others fly right, twisting and turning, a living, breathing mass that forms a wave here and a ribbon there, shifting into the shape of an undulating cloud. From the ground, the awkward Priggs watch and wonder at the sight of their communal flight.

"But, Indigo, how can they fly like that without crashing and falling from the sky?"

Indigo winks, and Robin winks back as together they swirl in an aerial dance. "Look in my eyes, and what do you see?"

"I am in you, and you are in me."

"And when we fly, what do we do?"

"We move as one Sprite, instead of as two."

"When two becomes four, and four becomes eight, you'll rise above fear and fly above hate. And when you fly at this new height, you'll cease to be Priggs and then become Sprites."

The Priggs, who had been taught to walk with their heads bowed in shame, for the first time look into one another's eyes. It is there that they see themselves for who they truly are. Now empowered by this new union, they unfold their wings and together rise in a churning wave, blending in motion with the gyration of the birds over the Lullwater.

CHAPTER FIFTEEN

Two suns have risen over Prospect Park—one peering through the silhouette of trees that fringe the shore while its twin is reflected on the surface of the pond. Marveling at the flock of Sprites who fly with new purpose, the former first husband kisses the former governor on the cheek. "Well, Winnie, shall we join them?"

"Oh, Winston, I'm not sure I can."

"Be brave, my dear, and we'll cross over together." He turns to Sage and adds, "We have an open invitation from your father, the Duke, who will be overjoyed to hear you are alive and well. And like me, I'm sure he hopes his foolishness can be forgiven."

Without a flap of his wings, Thistle flies into his father's open arms where wordlessly they embrace, holding each other tightly.

From under a pile of wet leaves and beetle dung emerges a squirming grub. "Told you, lad, it'd turn out all right. Just Nature taking her course. And if she can't get there this way, she'll go another."

"Yes, you did. You are a very wise grub."

"Indeed," says Winston. "Well, Winnie, no better time than now." Interlocking their fingers, he and his wife bend their knees before springing toward the sky, a sparkle of their radiance bouncing off a tin can in the cattails—under which is submerged a tiny, sleek boat.

Sage runs on all fours and dives into the pond. Paddling toward her sunken scull, she dips below the surface to release its single oar from a tangle of feathery algae, then pulls it onto dry land. As she nudges a spotted salamander from its hull, a wave of sound rolls over the Lullwater. Somewhere between a hum and a rumble, it is rising from a legion of creatures who hover above the lily pads—their wings like their legs are folded, and their hands with fingers curled inward, resemble rosebuds about to open.

"Who are they?" asks Thistle. "And what are they doing?"

"Those, my friend, are the Nohms. And they're meditating for peace."

Disrupting their harmony, another more discordant sound of grumbling and cursing rises from the Grobbs that wades toward the bank and climbs onto land fully bathed and bickering.

"No bitterroot, and it's all your fault!"

"My fault? The turtle got him, not me."

"I ordered you to detain it."

"And get my head bit off too, no way!"

Thistle, freed from the shame that clouded his life as a Prigg, explodes with what was once illegal laughter. Sage's brow twists with confusion. "What's so funny?"

"Eon the snapping turtle was Bitterroot's spy on the Lullwater. But it was Eon who put an end to him."

"I get it," chuckles Sage. "And from my study of history, I know that eventually all dictators are carried off and devoured by time."

"Will you all please quiet down," scolds the third head as she closes her eye, bringing together the fingertips of two hands to imitate the Nohms. "I'm trying to meditate."

Then from her lipless orifice a mesmerizing song of one syllable rises, calming even the other two heads above her who also shut their mouths and hum. At

143

peace, the Grobbs rises and floats above the water, adding a new line of harmony to the song of the Nohms. Meanwhile emerging from the Root System, two skeletal hands carry out the crystal encrusted trunk from which muffled voices emerge.

"Thou dropped it?"

"Thou made me."

"I made thee? But how?"

"Oh, I don't know, Cobweb, but we must find it now!"

On the ground the bones of Queen Zinnia set down her trunk, opening its lid to release two agitated Sprites. "Peaseblossom, attend and mark, for I do hear the morning lark."

"Alas, how can I face a new day's light when I have lost the Last Law of the Sprites!"

"The Last Law?" cries Thistle. "That's been a mystery since the beginning of the New Order."

"Twas written on a scroll by Zinnia our Queen."

"Now 'tis dissolved like dew and never to be seen."

When with a wagging finger the bones scold the Sprites, Peaseblossom bows her head.

"I dropped it in the river, and I feel so ashamed." As she stands trembling, Cobweb steps forward.

"Do not punish Peaseblossom, for I will take the blame!"

"Shame, blame," grumbles Grub. "Now there's a useless pair—don't waste yer time on 'em."

"But Zinnia gave it to me, and now it's gone!"

"Nothing in Nature's ever lost. In fact, it's been safe with us grubs all along."

"You know the Last Law?" utters Thistle in amazement.

"Come on, I'm a grub, and us grubs? We dig deep, we get dirty and we know the real deal."

"But how can this be?"

"When Zinnia got booted down to the Root System, my ancestor was her only friend. And so, she told the Last Law to her, and she passed it down to us."

"If ever there were a time to tell it, Grub, it's now!"

Grub raises himself from the ground, inhaling deeply through his spiracles. But when he exhales, the voice of Zinnia arises from his mandibles.

"Listen well, my Prince, to this the Last Law which henceforth shall be your first."

For a moment Thistle stands stunned and confused, until his wings flutter with an ancient recognition of his great-great grandmother the Queen.

"This above all: to thine own self be true, and it must follow, as the night the day, thou canst not then be false to any creature."

Looking perplexed, Thistle turns toward Sage. "But I don't understand."

"Think about it. If you're true to yourself, you're doing what's good for all Sprites. Doesn't your being well depend on their well-being?"

145

"Yes, that's true."

"And if you're being true to yourselves, you have to be true to all other creatures because everyone's well-being depends on them being well. That's how the world is supposed to work."

"Ah," says Thistle, "That is a better principle than all 1,999 laws combined!"

"And never forget in Nature, my Prince, this truth we hold to be self- evident. All are created equal."

"Oh, yes," replies Thistle, bowing his head. "We will remember."

"Well, lads, my job is done," says Grub in his own gravelly voice before inching back toward the tree. "It's up to you now. As for me, time t'molt. Remember, what Zinnia used to say—live free without fear!"

"Goodbye, Grub, we will," cries Thistle as Sage steadies the scull for him to board. Then paddling toward New Hobb, they join the Sprites, Nohms and the Grobbs who are crossing the pond, radiant in the early morning sun. Still on shore Peaseblossom and Cobweb kiss the Queen's hand before her bones with a bow and a wave return to their resting place in the roots of the elm. Shooting upward in unison the Sprites call out, "Hence, away! now all is well: One aloof stands sentinel."

Standing on the uppermost branch of the elm, Robin Goodfellow leans on the wing of the fox-sparrow that tilts its head to observe the chattering creature. "Now let all who have been freed—inspirit the Lullwater and Nethermead. And as our tale comes to an end, allow me to share this verse by a friend." Robin unravels a scroll to read to the sparrow and, indeed, all creatures within hearing.

"If we fairies have offended,
Think but this, and all is mended,
That you have but slumber'd here
While these visions did appear.
And this weak and idle theme,
No more yielding but a dream,
Gentles, do not reprehend:
if you pardon, we will mend:
And, as I am an honest Puck,
If we have unearned luck
Now to 'scape the serpent's tongue,
We will make amends ere long;
Else the Puck a liar call;
So, good night unto you all.
Give me your hands, if we be friends,
And Robin shall restore amends."
A Midsummer Night's Dream (5.2.413-428)

The End

GLOSSARY of PEOPLE, PLACES & SPRITES

Arden, Mary Born to a Wilmcote farming family in Warwickshire, England about 1537, Mary was the youngest of eight sisters. Her intelligence was so trusted that after his death, her father left her in charge of the family property. Opting for the new life of the merchant class, in 1556 she married a glove-maker and moved to Stratford-upon-Avon where within a few short years, he rose to be High Bailiff.

During those years, her first two children died in infancy, so when William was born, all her time and attention would have been focused on her only son. When after his birth the plague spread to Stratford, she returned with him to the family farm in Wilmcote. It was her words, songs and stories that would have been Will's first experience of the English language. And as historical records indicate that entrance to the local public-school required students to read, it is highly likely that with her hornbook, Mary taught her son the alphabet that one day he would shape into poems and plays—assisted perhaps by a Sprite or two.

Arden, Robert Will's grandfather was a successful husbandman whose 150-acre farm produced livestock, vegetables, milk, cheeses and its own beer. For a farmer of that era, he provided his family with a comfortable home that had feather beds and colorful painted cloths that hung on the walls. One can imagine young Will as a boy, marveling at their imagery which might have depicted scenes from the bible, mythology or local legend.

Cobweb and Peaseblossom Two of five fairies named in William Shakespeare's *A Midsummer Night's Dream,* several of whose lines from that play have found their way into the mouths of these modern-day Sprites in *A Legend of Now.* Just for the record the others are Mustardseed, Moth and Robin Goodfellow, also known as Puck.

Elm of the New Order A very real tree, dubbed the Camperdown Elm, is located on the Lullwater of Prospect Park and has a fascinating tale of its own. In 1872 the tree was given as a gift to the new public park designed by Frederick Law Olmstead and Calvert Vaux from the estate of the Earl of Camperdown of Scotland. Grown from a graft that could not be reproduced, this rare elm was sorely neglected and almost demolished in the 1960s until a literary champion came to its rescue. Modernist poet, Marianne Moore, wrote a poem in the elm's honor, drawing attention to its plight, which resulted not only in the restoration of the Camperdown Elm, but also the creation of a group called Friends of Prospect Park to protect all the trees rooted in the park's 585 acres.

Forest of Prospect Park Once a teaming woodland that took root about 8,000 years ago, today about 150 acres survive as the last surviving forest of Brooklyn.

Lullwater The Lullwater is part of a chain of waterways and ponds designed and carved into the landscape of the park. At the Lullwater, where the basin widens, the currents slow before flowing into Prospect Park Lake.

Nethermead This central meadow of Prospect Park is a popular place for Them and their Beasts to relax near the Lullwater. Located at a spot from which no outside buildings are visible—it is a prime site for the reintroduction of mythical species such as the Sprites, Hobbs, Nohms and the Grobbs—the Priggs now being extinct. As *A Legend of Now* largely takes place after dark and until dawn, these mythical creatures have free range to haunt the Lullwater.

Prospect Park This 585-acre park, which opened in 1867, was designed by Frederick Law Olmsted and Calvert Vaux to provide human beings in an increasingly industrialized world with an environment where they could connect with nature.

Robin Goodfellow (Puck) In Old and Middle English, puck meant simply demon; according to

Elizabethan lore this mythical character was known as a hobgoblin or household sprite who, depending on his mood, could help or harm, playing slightly malicious pranks on the locals. While his identity shifts through the ages and cultures, here Puck is described in *A Midsummer Night's Dream*. *(1.2.399-411)*

FAIRY:

Either I mistake your shape and making quite,
Or else you are that shrewd and knavish sprite
Called Robin Goodfellow. Are not you he
That frights the maidens of the villagery;
Skim milk, and sometimes labour in the quern
And bootless make the breathless housewife churn;
And sometime make the drink to bear no barm;
Mislead night-wanderers, laughing at their harm?
Those that Hobgoblin call you and sweet Puck,
You do their work, and they shall have good luck:
Are not you he?

PUCK:

Thou speakest aright;
I am that merry wanderer of the night.

Sprite a genre of mythical creatures who dwell on or near water with the Sprites of this legend inhabiting the environs of the River Avon.

Stratford-upon-Avon When this medieval village

was licensed by the government to be a marketplace, a High Cross was erected at the junction of High Street and Bridge Street where merchants, farmers and peddlers could trade. At the time we meet Will as a young father, hurrying home with his son Hamnet on his shoulders—the town would have had a population of about 2,000 residents.

Will Perhaps only the youngest readers might miss the clues that identify Will as William Shakespeare, the legendary author of 154 sonnets, numerous other poems and 38 dramas (as far as we know), including *A Midsummer Night's Dream* on which this overnight romp in the forest of Prospect Park is loosely based— with Will and the fairies speaking some memorable lines from that and one other play. Born in 1664 in Stratford-upon-Avon, Will was raised in his family's house located on Henley Street—a few miles from his mother's farm in Wilmcote. There as a child he would have heard stories of the local hobgoblins and fairies whose descendants now dwell in Prospect Park.

Wilmcote This rural hamlet, located north of Stratford-upon-Avon, is where Robert Arden farmed 150 acres with his eight oxen and, perhaps, the help of the Hobbs. And where in an old elm, Queen Zinnia and the Sprites resided until journeying to seek a place to establish the New Order of the World.

Dedication

To Ben, Mor & Elias

Nothing retains its form, new shapes from old.
Nature, the great inventor, ceaselessly contrives.
Ovid, circa 8 CE

The mouse goes into the miracle and turns into everything.
Elias T. Ressler, circa 1995

Live Free Without Fear